I0745255

SHAPESHIFTER

COVEN: BOOK 4

DAVID NETH

 Publishing

Shapeshifter
Coven, Book 4
Copyright © 2021 by David Neth
Batavia, NY

www.DavidNethBooks.com

ISBN: 978-1-945336-14-0
First Edition

Subscribe to the author's newsletter for updates and exclusive content:
DavidNethBooks.com/Newsletter

Follow the author at:
www.facebook.com/DavidNethBooks

ALSO BY DAVID NETH

<u>COVEN</u>
HARPY
SIREN
VALKYRIE
SHAPESHIFTER
SORCERER
WITCH (SHORT STORY)
ENCHANTRESS
ORACLE

<u>UNDER THE MOON</u>
THE FULL MOON
THE HARVEST MOON
THE BLOOD MOON
THE CRESCENT MOON
THE BLUE MOON

THE ART OF MAGIC

<u>FUSE</u>
ORIGIN
OMERTÁ
OBLIVION

<u>HEAT</u>
BLACK MAGNET
DUST STORM
THE GATEKEEPER

<u>STANDALONE</u>
ALL I EVER WANTED

CHAPTER 1

- OCTOBER 1988 -

Ruby Harding finished washing her face in the bathroom sink and reached for the towel on the rack beside her. She patted her face dry, looked in the mirror for any blemishes that needed attention, then turned off the bathroom light as she stepped into the hall.

At the top of the stairs, she stopped and listened for the sounds of movement below. Instead, she heard the TV and her husband's snores. He had fallen asleep on the couch *again*. They hadn't been married that long to be in a rut already, but here they were.

Ruby rolled her eyes and padded into the bedroom, where she had already turned on both bedside lamps and drawn the curtains. Pulling the blanket back, she crawled into bed.

SHAPESHIFTER

She was reading Stephen King's *Misery*. She'd slowly been working her way through his entire catalog for a few years now. The stories sometimes scared her so bad she had trouble sleeping. She figured she should probably stop reading these types of books before bed, but she couldn't help it. Horror books made her feel alive, which was more than could be said about her relationship with her husband as of late.

Ruby opened the book and got started on the next chapter. She was three pages in when she heard the floorboards creak from downstairs.

Finally, Eli is coming to bed, she thought. When she glanced at the clock, she couldn't help but feel a little disappointed. He usually stayed down there for another half hour, which gave her ample peace and quiet time by herself to read.

Okay, so maybe she didn't totally hate the fact that he fell asleep on the couch.

Turning back to her book, she read another half page before she heard the distinct murmur of voices from downstairs that were definitely not coming from the TV.

Ruby furrowed her brow and leaned forward in bed to try to catch a glimpse out the bedroom door, which stood ajar. She debated getting up and seeing who it was, but she was all warm and cozy between the sheets. Besides, if they were people talking, Eli likely knew who they were and the conversation wouldn't last long. She didn't think it was rude to stay in bed at this hour, anyway.

She leaned back and tried to get back into *Misery*, but two thoughts kept nagging at her.

That voice didn't sound familiar.

I didn't hear the door open.

Sticking the bookmark between the pages, Ruby set the book back down on the nightstand and tossed the blankets aside. She wouldn't be able to relax until she figured out whose voice it was and what they wanted. Even if she embarrassed herself by going down in a bathrobe, it would help her—

She stopped moving when she heard a loud thud from downstairs. Almost as if someone fell or a stack of books were dropped.

Determined that she needed to investigate, Ruby set her feet on the hardwood and began to rise when she heard footsteps coming up the stairs.

Her heart raced and her mind ran through all of the possibilities—expanding due to her love of horror books, which now served as a new way to terrorize her. Building up the courage to scope things out anyway, she rose to her feet and took several tentative steps to the door.

You're being silly, Ruby, she told herself. *There's no one down there. It was probably just Eli making a mess.* She crept closer to the door and jumped when her husband's face suddenly appeared in the darkness. She let out a quick yelp.

Instantly, her heart rate slowed as the irrational panic subsided. A moment later, her face turned to confusion as the embarrassment for the thoughts she had only moments ago set in.

"What was that noise?" she asked quickly to disguise her paranoia.

"It was the phone." He stepped to his dresser and began to pull off his clothes.

"I didn't hear it ring." She stood with her hands on her hips, still too anxious to crawl back into bed. "And who was calling at this hour anyway?"

"Prank caller." He pulled his belt out of his jeans and set it on the top of the dresser. "I told them to stop calling."

"And that thud?" she asked.

"The phone slipped out of my hands." He pulled off his jeans and dug something out of one of the pockets. Rather than hang them on the knob to wear tomorrow, he balled them up and tossed them on the floor beside the dresser.

"If you're done wearing those, couldn't you at least put them in the hamper?"

Eli turned and stepped toward her quickly, slipping his hand around her and tossing her onto the bed. Startled, she looked up at him as he crawled on top of her and began kissing her hungrily. He moved down to her neck and she became overwhelmed by lust, before the nagging feeling that something wasn't right made her push him away.

"Hold on, Eli," she said. "Just wait." She crawled up a little higher on the bed to put distance between them. "Where is this coming from?"

"Can't I kiss my wife?" he asked. "Maybe a little more too?"

"But we just did it two days ago." That was one way she knew they were in a rut: sex came like clockwork every Sunday. As if it was something to check off on a to-do list.

"So?" he asked. "I want you now."

Ruby smiled at the spontaneity. Eli took it as an invitation to continue and he started working at her neck again, kissing it in that spot that she liked.

Her eyes fluttered open for a moment and she caught of glimpse of him fishing for something behind him. She tried to ask what he was doing, but his mouth pressed against hers kept her from saying anything.

The feeling that something wasn't right came flying back to her. Above her, Eli pulled a pocket knife out of the waistband of his underwear. As he flicked the blade open, her eyes widened in fear and she immediately pushed at his chest in an attempt to free herself, but the weight of him held her in place.

Eli reached for her throat with his free hand. In an instant, his face changed from seductive to sinister as he swatted away her feeble attempts to free herself from his grip. Instead, he removed his hand from her throat and used it to press one of her hands against her side.

She swatted at him with her free hand, squirming and thrashing on the bed. But the way she was restrained left most of her torso exposed.

Shapeshifter

The perfect opportunity to jab the pocket knife into her once, twice, three times.

Ruby let out a shriek as the knife skewered through her. Eli adjusted his hand so it covered her mouth to muffle her screams. He delivered several more jabs, this time directly to her stomach.

Blood seeped out of her wounds, staining the white linens and pooling beneath her body. Still she fought to push him away; the pain not setting in. Her mind was focused on one thing only: get away.

But with each movement she made, her heart pumped more blood out of her, killing her faster as the panic took over. With her strength diminished, her movements slowed to a stop and she finally succumbed to her wounds.

Eli stood, his own heart racing, and looked down at his work. Grinning, he turned and stepped to the bathroom for a shower.

CHAPTER 2

Don't forget to read Chapters Four and Five in your textbook," Professor Roger Mitchell said at the end of class. "And more importantly, finish reading the Edith Wharton book! We'll be discussing it on Friday, so please be prepared. Have a nice day everyone!"

Kathy sat at her seat and scribbled out the homework at the top of the page in her notebook. If she learned anything in her nearly two months of college, it was to take notes on everything, especially the homework.

She just didn't think there'd be this much *reading*.

With most of the rest of the class filing out faster than she thought humanly possible, Kathy stuffed her books back into her bag while her mind raced with everything she had to do.

Shapeshifter

The reading Roger just assigned would take her several hours. At least they were having a discussion on it and not a reflection essay. That added even more to her workload, which was already threatening to break her. The good thing was, she actually liked this Early American Literature class.

Her Spanish 101 class, on the other hand, made her tense up every time she even thought about it. Learning a foreign language never interested her, but it was one of the few entry-level classes left so close to the start of the semester—since she registered only two weeks before classes started—and both her advisor and Samantha said that getting the foreign language class out of the way early was a good plan.

Of course, neither of them had to do the actual work.

Hauling her heavy backpack up onto her shoulder, Kathy felt it smack into someone behind her when she got it on her back.

"Oh, I'm so sorry!" she said when she saw Harry, one of her classmates, recoil the arm she had hit.

"Do you have enough books in there?" He offered a perfect smile that revealed dimples on both sides of his cheeks.

Kathy noted how cute he was her first day, but there were several things holding her back from pursuing Harry. Chief among them was that she was here to learn, not find a boyfriend. If she started blurring that line with boys, she'd lose all focus.

"Sorry," she said. "Would you believe I'm only taking two

classes?" She pointed to the door. "Mind if we walk and talk? I have to get to work soon."

Harry stood back and held out his arm for Kathy to go first. She maneuvered out between the tight row of tables and into the hallway, which very much resembled a barn.

Porreco College was fairly new, having been a farmstead prior to its first classes only the previous year. Despite it's suburban location, there was no denying that the school still had remnants of its more rural past. Namely, the two silos that stood high above all the other buildings on the property.

It made for a quirky anecdote and a notable landmark to look for the few times Kathy drove.

"So I was wondering if you'd like to study together sometime," Harry said.

"For this class? I mean, it's just a bunch of reading, mostly. And I'm already kind of a slow reader and this stuff isn't exactly a *light* read."

He chuckled and pushed open the door at the end of the hallway that led out to the sidewalk. He held it back for Kathy to step through. "Okay, so maybe disguising my intent as *studying* was a bad idea. How about a drink, then?"

"A drink?" she asked, then blurted, "Are you even old enough to drink?"

That was another downside to her starting classes. She was twenty-one taking freshmen classes while most of her classmates were still only eighteen, having started college right after high school. Like most people did. She didn't think three years would make that big of a difference, but in many of the discussions they had had in class about the reading, she usually felt so *old*. Of course, with what she and Samantha dealt with as witches, Kathy knew she was more mature than most twenty-one-year-olds.

Harry laughed again. "Okay, so we can't *go out* for a drink, but if you're cool with it, we could hang in my parents' garage. They won't care."

Kathy pulled the sleeves down on her sweater as they made it out to the parking lot, where the occasional gust of wind brought a chill to the otherwise sunny day.

"As tempting as indulging in underage drinking is, I think I'm going to have to pass," she said. "I just have a lot going on right now with this class and work and my sister's getting married soon."

"You still haven't mentioned a boyfriend," he pushed with a smirk. "Are you seeing anyone?"

Immediately, Kathy's mind went to Milo. While what they had was nothing official, the two of them had been getting together at least once a week for the last couple of months. Surprisingly, their encounters were in the daylight, even though they met at a nightclub. In her experience, guys she met in the wee hours of the night never quite looked—or acted—the same once she got them in the light and introduced them to her life with responsibilities.

Not that she usually had a ton of responsibilities, other than magical ones.

"Um…sort of," she said to Harry. Milo certainly wasn't her boyfriend, but it would be a bit of a slap in the face to him if she suddenly started seeing someone else too. As far as she knew, Milo wasn't even talking to any other girls. He had a lot going on too.

"So is that a maybe?"

Kathy glanced at her watch. "I have to get to the bus stop if I'm going to make it to work on time, I should—"

"I could drive you."

And show him that she worked at the mall, thus proving that she wasn't as sophisticated as she just made herself sound? Pass.

"That's really sweet of you, but I don't want to burden you. I think I'm going to stick with the bus." She started walking backward across the parking lot to the bus stop on W 38th Street.

"It's no burden!" Harry called out as she put more distance between them.

She pretended she didn't hear and waved. "We'll talk Friday at our next class!"

"Wait, Kathy!"

She let out a heavy sigh and stopped moving, their conversation even more awkward now that there was nearly ten feet between them.

"I was hoping to invite you to a Halloween party this

weekend," he admitted.

Halloween was Monday, but all the parties were this weekend. With everything going on, Kathy had nearly forgotten about the holiday, which was almost like a witch sin.

"It's at a friend of mine's house," he went on. "We don't need to call it a date or anything like that, but I'd like to see more of you. Outside of class."

Kathy stammered and looked back to the bus stop. The next bus would arrive soon and she really didn't want to run with her heavy backpack. That would make standing at work for the next eight hours even more dreadful.

"I have to go," she said. "I'm sorry! We'll talk Friday!" Turning, she walked toward the bus stop faster than she usually did, cursing herself the whole way for making the entirety of that conversation with Harry uncomfortably awkward.

CHAPTER 3

Samantha shut the door to her car and slung her bag over her shoulder when she got home. It had been a long day. She walked down to the sidewalk and took in the large mature trees whose leaves had turned to beautiful warm fall colors. It was about the only bit of reprieve she'd have all day. She had a million things to do at work and the last thing she needed was the headache of her future mother-in-law coming to her house for the first time to plan the wedding.

Or rather, *take over* planning the wedding.

The whole way home, Samantha had been forming rebuttals to snide comments she assumed Steven's mother would make. And yet those comebacks would probably only venture as far as the tip of her tongue.

Across the street, Eli Harding carried the back half of a recliner down his driveway. The bottom half of the chair sat at the curb. When he dropped the pieces together, he smiled and waved at Samantha.

"Hi Eli," she called out to him. "How's the new place?" Eli and his wife, Ruby, were clients of her firm. They were roughly the same age as Samantha and she loved the idea that another young couple had moved onto the street.

Eli crossed over to her side and stood at the curb beside Samantha. "Still needs some work, but we're excited to get our hands dirty. Ruby's got all kinds of ideas for projects from those home magazines." He rolled his eyes and smiled. "Whatever makes her happy."

"'Happy wife, happy life' has a grain of truth to it," she admitted.

He laughed. "Hey, you're about to find that out for yourself, aren't you? Big day's coming up."

"Not for a couple more months," Samantha said. "Actually, Steven and his mother are supposed to be over today to work on some more plans, so I should probably—"

"Do you have a lot to work on?"

She shrugged. "I guess. Kathy and I picked out a couple dresses a few weeks ago. Still haven't pulled the trigger on any one in particular."

"Isn't that usually the first thing you do?"

"I'm not too picky about it. Honestly, I'm only going to wear it one day, so the better deal I get on it the happier I'll be. And I got a pretty good deal."

"Geez, I think I married the wrong woman." He laughed.

Samantha rolled her eyes. "Don't say that! Ruby's great."

"Of course, yeah. I love her. She's definitely the one for me and all that, but sometimes I just wish she'd be able to cut back on her spending, you know?"

She furrowed her brow, thinking back to their tax returns. From what she remembered, Eli was the one who spent more money than Ruby did. But then, Samantha saw a lot of files come across her desk. She could've just been remembering wrong.

The two neighbors both turned when Steven pulled into the driveway behind Samantha's car. They watched as he got out and trotted over to them.

"Sorry, had a hard time getting out of the office," he said. Turning to Eli, he thrust out his hand. "Hi, I'm Steven, Samantha's fiancé."

Eli greeted him, but looked to Samantha. "Oh, so this is Mr. Right? Well, I'll make sure to stand out of your way." He laughed and patted Steven hard on the shoulder. "Geez, do you live at the gym?"

Steven laughed along politely as Samantha looked her fiancé up and down. Steven looked good, but he was by no means a hugely muscular guy. Her eyes went up to Steven's face and saw just how uncomfortable he looked.

"Eli and his wife, Ruby, are some of my clients." Samantha pointed across the street. "They just moved in right over there."

"Oh okay." Steven nodded to the recliner at the curb. "You're not throwing that chair away, are you? Looks comfortable."

Eli waved it off. "Nah, it's got a big tear in the back. Damaged in the move, you know?"

"I've had that happen," Steven said. "As if you don't spend enough money when you move, right?"

"I know!" he said with his eyebrows raised. "I mean, it's completely out of control. First you try to get rid of all your stuff so there's extra garbage fees and that kind of thing. Then you have to shell out all this money for a moving truck and some people to help you get all your furniture out of your old place and into your new one. Then you have to buy more furniture and curtains and linens and oh my God, it just doesn't stop!"

"Well, hey, next time you need help moving, just let me know," Steven offered.

Eli burst out laughing and patted Steven on the arm again. "This guy! Kicking me out of the neighborhood already!"

"No, that's not—"

"I'm just teasing, I'm just teasing." He waved his hand at Steven to quiet him. "No, I appreciate your confidence. Offering your help *after* the work's done."

This time, Steven remained quiet, his face flaring red once more. Samantha could tell he didn't know what to say.

From beside him, she smiled politely. "Well, it was nice

talking to you, Eli. But we need to get ready for when Steven's mom comes later."

"Oh sure," Eli said. "You've got a lot of work to do! Hey, before you go, I just wanted to invite you guys to a little Halloween party Ruby and I are having on Saturday. I know it's a few days early, what with Halloween being on Monday and all, but we figured more people would come this way."

Samantha and Steven exchanged looks, wordlessly trying to negotiate a reason why they couldn't come. Finally, Samantha gave in to the inevitable.

"Sure, sounds fun."

"Yeah, it'll be a blast," Eli said. "Think of it as a housewarming party of sorts—but no gifts! We're doing this to meet the neighbors. We're not trying to hold our hand out or anything like that."

"Of course not," Steven said.

"Invite anyone you want," Eli went on. "Your sister—Kathy, is it?"

Samantha nodded.

"She's welcome, even her gentleman friend if she's got one. Bring them all!"

"She's always got a gentleman friend," Steven said with a grin.

Samantha smacked his arm as a warning. "I'll let her know."

"The more the merrier!" Eli said. "Hey, it was nice talking to you. You two take it easy now, okay? I'll see you later!" He offered another wave and then jogged across the street and back to his house.

Steven looked at Samantha. "He's…"

"I know. But we can go to the party and play nice. With them living across the street, he's obviously not going anywhere."

He glanced back at Eli's house. "Unfortunately."

"I'm more concerned about your mother coming over and taking over the wedding." Samantha jabbed her finger into his chest playfully. "That means you and I have some decisions to make before she gets here. Let's go."

CHAPTER 4

As tedious as refolding clothes was, Kathy welcomed the mindless task at work. It made her feel accomplished straightening out the tables that customers had destroyed as they rifled through for their size. And it gave her time to slow down and think, which she found she didn't have much time for nowadays.

Her life had completely changed in the last couple months. She never thought she'd be taking college classes, working in retail, or getting offers for dates from different men.

Well, that last one hadn't changed.

What *had* changed was her lack of interest in both Milo and Harry. She liked them both. They were friendly and especially Milo made her laugh. But they weren't like Jeremy.

She missed him.

Not that it mattered. They had both moved on. At least, the fact that Jeremy hadn't called her told her that he had moved on. She needed to move on too. Although, judging by how much her life had changed in the last couple months, it could be argued that she *had* moved on. Still, she couldn't help but feel like she hadn't made much progress at all in her life.

After straightening out the table she was working on, she picked up an empty hanger from the floor and reorganized the sizes on one of the racks. When she looked up, she saw Milo smile at her as he came through the mall entrance.

"Hey." He walked up and tried to give her a kiss, but she turned her head and his lips landed on her cheek.

Why do I do stuff like this? Milo is really sweet and it was nice of him to come visit. A quick peck would be okay, right?

"Hey," she said back.

"You okay to go on your break or do you need to wait a little bit?" He stuffed his hands in his pockets and took a step back, clearly getting the message that she wanted him to back off.

"I suppose I could go on my break now." She offered a smile to try to ease the tension, but she knew it was a feeble attempt. "Give me a sec."

After telling her manager and clocking out, Kathy pulled off her name tag and followed Milo back out to the mall and toward the food court.

"How's work?" he asked as they walked.

"Boring," she said. "But you're a nice surprise." She wasn't lying about that. He was good company, but she still couldn't see him as "boyfriend" company.

"I had some shopping to do," he told her. "Figured I'd grab something to eat with you before I collected a million bags."

"Good thinking," she said. "I might get jealous. Actually, no. I think working here has ruined the mall for me."

He laughed.

When they arrived at the food court, they both ordered—fast food, since that was basically the only option—and claimed a table by one of the fake palm trees. It offered them a small bit of privacy.

"So how was work for you?" She picked up her burger and took a bite. Immediately, she set it down and pulled off the pickles.

"Busy," he said. "We've got a few sidewalk updates going in on different streets around the city. We're finishing up a water line replacement over on 9th. Just trying to wrap things up before the winter hits."

Milo worked for the City of Erie in the Public Works department. It was an area of government she hadn't cared much about before she met him, but now she found herself asking him the scoop on different development projects happening because there was a good chance he knew about them.

"You working out in the field?"

"A bit," he said. "Mostly supervision, but it was nice to get away from my cubicle."

Kathy pointed up to the skylights. "This is about as much daylight as I get—and it's fading."

The days were getting shorter, meaning that it was usually dark by time she got home from working at the store. That made getting homework done harder and harder as the semester progressed. Fall was her favorite season, but her impossibly long to-do list was ruining it for her.

As if reading her mind, Milo asked, "How are your classes?"

"The one is really good," she said. "I like it. It's a lot of work, but I'm managing. But Spanish? Forget it."

"The other one is an English one, right?"

She nodded and licked ketchup off her thumb. "Mm-hmm. Early American Literature."

"I haven't taken either of those since high school," he said. "I admire you for going back."

"Yeah," she murmured and started on her fries.

Words of encouragement like that—while well-intentioned—only made Kathy feel worse for being so discouraged about school and the workload. Everyone was telling her this was what she should be doing, but as much as she tried, she just didn't care for it. Not in the same way she thought she ought to.

Discussing the readings in class wasn't bad, but she didn't want to write the paper about it. Nor did she think it was healthy to maintain the lightning-fast reading speed she was expected to accomplish all semester.

And this was only an introductory course. There were people who were going on for higher degrees. Clearly, they were different people than she was. She felt like she wasn't cut out for it. Not like Samantha.

"What's the matter?" Milo asked, picking up on her tone.

She shrugged. "I just feel like I'm still unsure of what to do with my life."

"That's okay. You're still young. College will help you figure it out."

"Will it, though?" she asked. "They told me what classes to take. There were only a few options left and I didn't care for most of them. I haven't gone through any sort of career exploration or anything. And even if I did and I *knew* what I wanted to do, the fact of the matter is that I still need to work to live, so I need to juggle work and school and *paying* for school all at once."

"I thought your sister was helping you out with the cost?"

Kathy sighed. "She is, but I wish she didn't need to. We could use the money elsewhere." She had a sinking suspicion that Samantha was pushing for a small wedding to save on costs. Costs that probably went to Kathy's tuition.

"Didn't you say you helped pay for her school when she went?"

Kathy regretted telling him that, but it only came up

because he suggested she quit working at the store while she was in school. That slipped out the last time she was complaining about college. What were these classes doing to her? They were fundamentally changing who she was as a person and she didn't care for it.

"I did say that," Kathy said. "But Samantha is much more suited for college and a professional life than I am."

"That's not true," he said. "You're just green. You'll get the hang of it. It's been two months, cut yourself some slack."

"I just feel like I'm wasting Samantha's money," she went on. "She knew what she wanted to do when she started school. She set a goal and she reached it. I feel like I'm just floundering."

"A lot of people feel that way," he said. "Now it's time for you to go through it. But you'll figure it out. It's your journey, so it's something *you* need to figure out for yourself."

She clasped her hands together and sat back. "Yeah, I guess you're right."

"What are you doing after work?" he asked.

Kathy shrugged and reached for her drink to take a sip. "I would love to go home and sleep, but I have reading to start on."

"Why don't you take tonight off," he suggested. "Start fresh tomorrow. Come over to my place and I'll help you relax."

"Milo, I can't." She knew exactly what he was implying—and he had been patient—but she wasn't there yet with him. Truthfully, she wasn't sure she was ever going to be at that level of intimacy with him. Better to deflect. "I have a pile of homework and I'm not going to be able to relax until I make some progress on it."

"I understand," he said. "What about tomorrow?"

"Uh…sure. Tomorrow will work. I don't have class and I'm off tomorrow, so I'm all yours when you get out of work."

"Perfect!" His eyes lit up. "You can spend the day doing homework and then relax in the evening with me."

She offered a tight smile. "I should get back to work. Thanks for spending my break with me."

"Of course. I love seeing you."

CHAPTER 5

O kay, so it's agreed?" Samantha asked. "We'll have the wedding at the Belle Valley Fire Hall? The wedding, the reception—everything?"

Steven sat beside her at the dining room table, papers with price quotes from different vendors scattered around them. Samantha had a yellow legal pad in front of her, where she was listing all of the costs and important dates to remember. In the top right corner, she also had a to-do list that had several things crossed off.

"Samantha, relax," he said in response. "We've already discussed this."

"Yes, but we haven't booked it yet. I don't want your mother to come swooping in and changing all of our plans. This is *our* wedding. We need to decide together."

"You're worrying too much about her."

Samantha shook her head. "She's already turned her nose up at my dress choices, at the catering, *and* the photographer. And you haven't backed me up on any of those. So yes, I'm worried."

"I haven't even seen any of the dresses you're considering!" he said. "Besides, she raised valid points about all of them. The catering tasted great, but was kind of expensive. And she heard from my cousin that the photographer was drunk for most of her wedding, so a lot of the pictures were blurry."

He was probably drunk because your mother was telling him what to do too, Samantha thought, but kept it to herself.

"I'm just saying, you and I are the ones who get the final decision."

"And we will," he assured. "But you need to at least listen to her."

"Then she needs to listen to me too," she said. "And I need you to back me up."

"Isn't that kind of putting me in the middle?"

Samantha shot him a look. "When it comes to our wedding, who do you think you should be supporting? Your mother or the woman who is about to make a lifelong commitment to you?"

He didn't answer.

"Steven, I'm not asking for some over-the-top extravagant

wedding. I want it to be small, intimate. And I'm *not* backing down from that. Hell, I don't even care if we just go down to city hall and get married and come back here and have a cookout."

Quietly, he murmured, "I'd care."

Samantha let out a sigh. She knew she was overcompensating for his mother taking over things by being too controlling herself. She wanted to make decisions together with Steven, but the fact remained: he treated everything his mother said as gold and would change his opinion based on hers.

"I'm sorry if it seems like I'm barreling through without you," she said. "I just feel like I'm fighting to get a say with all of these decisions. Or having to justify my decisions."

"Samantha, if you really don't care about the size of the wedding, then why is this such an issue?"

She opened her mouth to reply, then closed it again as she thought better of it. After giving it some thought, she treaded carefully in an attempt to explain her position. Dealing with family ties and disrupting traditions that no longer worked was a delicate art. Especially when she was trying not to piss off anyone she was about to become family with.

"The wedding doesn't matter to me as much as our marriage does," she started.

He nodded. "I agree. But I don't see—"

"And the way you're letting your mother challenge everything I say about the wedding makes me afraid that she's going to dictate our entire marriage as well."

"That's not going to happen."

"You said the same thing about the wedding planning, and yet here we are," she countered. "I'm not trying to make your mother the enemy. I'm just trying to make you see that you and I are supposed to be partners. If we can't even figure out how to work together to plan a party for one day, how are we going to be able to navigate a life together? Especially considering how eccentric mine can be."

Steven took her hands in his and leaned forward to kiss her forehead. "Take a deep breath. Relax. I hear what you're saying and I'll try to do better to support you."

"Thank you."

"But I think there might be more going on here," he added.

"Like what?"

"Well," he said slowly. Carefully. "Maybe this wedding planning is bringing up old feelings about your parents."

Samantha pulled away from him. "You think I'm jealous your mother is here and mine isn't?"

"Not jealous, just…sad." He shrugged. "I don't know. I can't imagine it's easy. Getting married is a big deal, especially for a girl."

"Getting married is a big deal, period. Whether you're a girl or a boy. And besides, I've made peace with the fact that my mother wouldn't ever see me walk down the aisle or hold my child or any of that." Her voice quivered, suggesting that she hadn't actually come to terms with it.

But the truth was, even though she had come to accept it, it still made her sad to think that she would no longer be able to turn to her mother for advice or support. That her children would never know their grandmother.

Not that Samantha had known her mother long. She was young when her mother passed, but you never stop needing your mom. Even if she's dead.

"She's been gone a long time," Samantha finally said. "So no, that hasn't come up until just now."

Steven stared at his hands, fidgeting with a spare pen. He looked up through his brow at her. "And what about your father?"

"What about him?"

"He hasn't been gone a long time," he said. "And he was there for you growing up."

"Until he wasn't," Samantha snapped. "Look, if this is your way to try to convince me to track him down, you're wasting your breath."

"Couldn't you magically find him somewhere?"

"You don't think we tried that? When he left, that's the first thing we did. Nothing. When we were so short on cash that Kathy couldn't go on her high school senior trip with her friends, I tried to reach out again. Nothing. When we were buying the week-old bread at the grocery store because we couldn't afford a fresh loaf, I reached out again. *Nothing.* And when I graduated college, I didn't even bother. So you think he's going to suddenly show up just because I'm getting married? It doesn't matter what he says anymore. His actions have proved that he doesn't give a damn about us. So why would I waste my energy on him?"

Steven swallowed and licked his lips. "Samantha, I'm sorry. I didn't—"

"Just drop it." She wiped tears away from her eyes.

The pain of losing her father hurt worse than losing her mother. At least with her mom, there was a reason she was gone. With her father, things had been good. They were fun. They struggled, but they managed. He taught her and Kathy how to use their magic. He taught her how to craft potions. They hunted down evil together.

And then he was gone. Without a real explanation. Without any trail to follow or any indication that he'd be back. And he stayed gone.

Samantha sucked in a shuddering breath and looked back down at the legal pad. With wet eyes, she asked, "So Belle Valley, yes or no?"

Steven studied her, worried that he made a mistake by bringing up her parents. He opened his mouth to respond, but the ringing doorbell cut him off.

CHAPTER 6

- July 1982 -
Rochester, NY

Ian was having one of those dreams where he was being chased by someone. The fear, racing heart, even the sweat—it all felt so real. He was running down a dark street, each house he passed without any lights on. As if sending a message to keep out. No refuge here.

Inherently, he knew it was the middle of the night. Probably also because he was barefoot and only wearing a pair of loose-fitting shorts.

Despite it all, the summer heat was insurmountable. He felt himself gasping for breath, choking as he ran. He knew it was all a dream, but still, every bit of it felt tangible, real.

But there was a light at the end of the proverbial tunnel. Ian figured the sunrise must be coming soon. He could hear the faint chirps of a bird. Irregular, but present.

In the dream, he ran faster, trying to outrun his pursuer, whoever he was. Every time he felt like he was gaining some ground, something strange happened that kept Ian back. The ground shifted into sand, slowing his pace. Or he stumbled over a rock on the ground, causing him to watch for any other tripping hazards in his wake.

Rounding a corner, Ian took cover in the crook of a doorway to catch his breath, which was getting harder and harder the more he ran.

Still, that bird chirped.

Amazingly, he didn't have a cramp. At least that way he could start running again when his breath caught up to him.

And yet, the longer he stood there, the more it seemed like his breathing was getting worse. More challenging. Was this another element of his dream?

Ian decided to start running again, this time heading in the direction from where he came.

Darting out from the entryway, he nearly collided with his pursuer, who grabbed him by his arms with a fierce grip. The adrenaline coursing through Ian's body was very much there, even despite the dream.

Just as the attacker presented a knife and raised it to Ian's throat, the chirping of that bird grew louder, the oppressive heat too much to ignore.

Lurching to his side in his bedroom, Ian woke up and

immediately began coughing.

The entire room was filled with smoke. The chirping was his fire alarm in the next room. It didn't immediately wake him because the door was closed.

Rising to his feet, Ian rushed to the bedroom door—trying to convince himself that the floor beneath him didn't feel *that* hot. He was on the second story, so if the fire started below, he was toast.

Through the window, Ian saw flashing lights. He poked his head out and waved to get their attention. He tried to yell, but it was useless. The smoke had coated his throat so much that speaking was impossible. Instead, he hung out as far as he dared—there was nothing beneath the window to step out onto—and waved his arms out.

The air was refreshing and he considered jumping, but the cement driveway below him spoke only of broken bones.

Out on the street, someone pointed at him. For the first time since he woke up, he felt a brief sense of relief. He was about to be rescued.

Unless he could rescue himself.

Turning back to the bedroom door, he swung it open to try to see if he could just walk outside. Instead, he was struck in the face with a burst of flame that lurched toward the open window.

Ian screamed, feeling his throat tearing apart, and fell backward toward his bed. His face was on fire. The pain excruciating.

He slammed against the wall and sunk to the floor as the fire ravaged his face. Then he had a thought: his blankets. If he could feel his way to his bed, he could smother the fire on his face.

But as he reached out to step further, he heard a crackling, then a loud crash as the ceiling caved in from above, trapping him beneath and enveloping him in flame.

Now his whole body was on fire.

He screamed again, his throat tearing apart even worse now. His body thrashed in the fiery debris, scratching his charred skin against splinters, nails, and electrical wires.

Somehow, faintly, he heard muffled voices through it all.

"Here!" he tried to yell out. "I'm here!" But just like the dream, his voice was incapable of making a sound that would carry in the roar of the fire.

He would need another plan.

With another shriek of pain, Ian shot his hand through a hole in the debris and out toward the space where his bedroom once was. He waved it around and after a minute, he felt a hot glove grasp it.

"We're here!" came the muffled voice. "We need to lift this debris off of you, but we have you. There's an ambulance waiting for you outside. Just hold tight!"

Over the next several minutes that carried out like an eternity, the firemen lifted burning boards, plaster, and other makings of the house, tossing them to the side.

By time everything was lifted off of him, Ian could only feel the heat of the flames on his skin. His eyelids had been melted shut.

As one of the firemen lifted him gently, Ian could only groan as the sensation of someone touching him grated at his skin. Like someone was ripping him apart.

The last thing he remembered before he passed out was the frigid night air as they escaped the burning house he had once called his home. The air that he had been complaining was too hot only a few hours earlier when he went to bed, not knowing that his life would be significantly altered the next time he woke up.

CHAPTER 7

Mary, hi." Samantha stood aside and held the door open for her future mother-in-law.

"Hello, dear." Her voice was emotionless until she spotted Steven and her face lit up. "Oh, and there's my boy!" She stepped forward and wrapped her arms around Steven as if she hadn't seen him in years. When they pulled apart, she took off her coat and held it out to Samantha. "Is there someplace I can hang this? I don't see a hook anywhere. We have a spot right by the door for coats and shoes at my house. It's very helpful to keeping down clutter, dear."

"Yes, we have one too." Samantha forced a smile and pointed behind the door where the coat rack was.

"Oh, I see," Mary murmured. "Tucked away for guests. How

cumbersome."

Samantha closed the front door and took Mary's coat, which she hung on the coat rack.

Mary wandered into the living room and looked around.

"What do you think, Mom?" Steven asked. "Isn't this place amazing? It has all the original woodwork and that fireplace is real cozy."

"Yes, cozy's the word for the whole house, isn't it?" Mary looked around expressionless. She pointed to a corner of the ceiling in the living room. "Original plaster, I see. Yes, that's a problem with these old houses. They're more likely to crack and break."

Samantha looked up and noticed the faintest dip in the plaster, which she hadn't even noticed until it was pointed out. Of course Steven's mother would find the lone imperfection in the room.

"I wish the sun would stay out later," Mary said. "It seems very dark in here."

"It *is* October," Steven said. "Halloween is Monday."

"Creeps up faster each year, doesn't it?" Mary said.

"Let's sit down and we can start digging in to the wedding plans." Samantha motioned to the dining room. "Mary, do you want anything to drink?"

Even though their relationship hadn't changed much since they first met back in July, Steven's mother had warmed up enough to Samantha to allow her to call her Mary. That was an improvement in Samantha's book. Much better than referring to her as "Mrs. Harper" or worse, "Steven's mom."

"Perhaps some cocoa or hot tea," Mary suggested as she settled into a chair at the table—the one Samantha had been sitting in. She shivered. "I see why you light that fire often. I feel a chill. Is there a draft in here?"

Samantha bit her lips together and squeezed Steven's arm hard, silently communicating with him that his mother was already pushing her buttons.

"I'll get you some tea, Mom," he said. "Any preference?"

Mary waved it off. "Oh, you know me. I'm not picky."

Samantha raised her eyebrows and took a seat across from her. She pulled the legal pad she had been keeping notes on over to her side, but it was too late. Mary had already seen it.

"The Belle Valley Fire Hall?" she asked with disgust. "Is that really where you're holding the wedding?"

"We were actually discussing that just before you arrived," Samantha said. "The wedding won't be too big. We've narrowed down the guest list to about seventy-five people, but I think that might even be able to be whittled down a bit."

"Oh, no, I can't let you get married at a fire hall," Mary said. "My son deserves something with more class."

"What did you have in mind?" Samantha asked, feeling her jaw tighten with stress.

Steven appeared in the doorway as he waited for the kettle to begin boiling.

"My brother is a member of the Lawrence Park Golf Club." Mary noticed Steven and added, "You know, Uncle Tony. Anyway, they have a beautiful dining room that can easily fit two hundred people. It's right on Lake Erie. Oh, it's just gorgeous!"

"We don't have two hundred guests," Samantha said. "And isn't that a little out of our price range?" She looked up at Steven for help.

Mary waved it off. "Oh, don't worry about that. If you decide to have it at the golf course, Marty and I can throw in a little extra. And we can find more people to invite to fill the room."

"But we've already narrowed down the guest list," Samantha said. "If we add more people, the cost of catering will go up."

"Oh, the golf course will want you to use their catering so those figures will change anyway."

Samantha gathered the papers scattered around the table. "So we're changing the venue, the guest list, *and* the catering? Hmm." She shot a look at Steven.

"Hey, Mom, is green tea okay?"

"Yes, that's fine, dear." Mary reached for a paper before Samantha could pull it away. "Oh, cake tasting! That's always so much fun—but bad for the waistline. Samantha, dear, perhaps you should consider opting out of that. You want to make sure you can fit into your wedding dress—when you find a good one."

"I'll fit just fine, thanks."

"Sugar, Mom?" Steven asked, exchanging looks with Samantha. She stared back with fury in her eyes. They had just talked about this. If this was his idea of supporting her, than clearly their talk had accomplished nothing.

"No thanks, dear," Mary said. "I want to make sure *I* fit into my dress on your wedding too."

"Well, you still have two and half months to lose weight," Samantha snapped.

Steven shot her a look, but she ignored him.

"We'll have to look into the golf course," Samantha said, knowing full well she had no intentions of changing the venue. Whether it was out of financial worry or spite, she wasn't certain. "But with the wedding so close, it might already be booked."

"We can do some finagling," Mary said. "My brother has been a member for years, I'm sure they'll make an exception for his nephew. Besides, late January is an odd time to have a wedding, so they might even have an opening already."

"We'll have to think about it," Samantha said.

They had chosen late January because Samantha thought it might mean prices for everything would be cheaper. She was wrong, but at this point, they already had invitations mocked up and she really liked the idea of a winter wedding.

"So where are we doing the cake testing?" Mary studied the flyer. "Oh, this bakery is delicious. A bit pricey, but if you're going with a cheap venue, you should at least splurge on the food. Make it at least a little enjoyable for your guests."

Samantha forced a smile. "Our guests will be happy to be there simply to see us get married. I don't want to invite people just to get more gifts."

Too far.

Mary set the paper down and turned to her. "Are you implying that I would invite people solely as a hand-out?"

"Tea's ready!" Steven announced loudly as he carried over a mug and set it in front of his mother. In his haste, he spilled some on his hand and winced.

"Thank you for being so considerate, dear," Mary said. "It's good to know there are still kind people in your generation." She cast Samantha a look as she took a sip.

"You know what?" Samantha started, but the abrupt opening of the front door cut her off.

"I'm home—oh, hello." Kathy flashed a smile at Mary when she stepped into the dining room. "I'm Kathy, Samantha's sister."

"Ah, yes, you're the one with countless jobs." Mary offered Kathy a limp hand. "Good for you, dear. Follow that spirit while you still have your looks."

Kathy held her smile. "Well, aren't you charming?" She stepped to the kitchen. "I'm just going to grab something to eat real quick and I'll be out of your hair. I have a ton of homework to get to."

"Excuse me," Samantha said before getting up to follow her

sister into the kitchen.

"Your future mother-in-law is a real peach," Kathy murmured once they were alone.

"Try planning a wedding with her," Samantha said. "And Steven's been no help. He better be talking to her now about her snide comments." She crossed her arms and huffed in the direction of the dining room. "Anyway, how was your day? I need time to decompress before I go back in there."

Kathy pulled a yogurt out of the refrigerator and reached for a spoon in the drawer. "My day was all right. Class in the morning, got homework—more reading, surprise-surprise. Then I went to work and Milo stopped in on my break to have an early dinner with me."

"That was nice."

"Yeah, it was." Kathy peeled off the lid and mixed up her yogurt. "He's just not quite setting off all those bells in me, you know?"

"Alarm bells? That'd be a good thing."

"No, like…attraction bells, or whatever."

"So break up with him."

"But he's nice and there is *some* attraction there," Kathy said. "I mean, we definitely had chemistry when we met at the club."

"That was different, though. This is reality."

Kathy shrugged. "I think it's me. I don't know what's going on. I mean, I practically pushed Jeremy away—"

"He wasn't exactly 'Boyfriend of the Year,' either," Samantha cut in.

"True, but then what's the deal with me and Milo? He's here. He likes me. He's trying. And I'm just losing interest."

"Kathy, you've got a lot going on right now. Your classes are taking up a lot of your time and I don't think it's selfish to say that you want to take a break from Milo so you can focus on school. Take care of yourself before you try to take care of someone else."

"Maybe."

"I know school wasn't your first choice, but I'm proud of you for sticking with it," Samantha said. "Keep it up and soon enough, we'll both have degrees and good jobs and life will be better."

"Yeah." Kathy picked at what was left of her yogurt.

"Oh, before I forget, I talked to Eli Harding, from across the street."

"When'd you see him?"

"He was outside when I got home and he walked over," Samantha explained. "Anyway, he said he's having a Halloween-slash-housewarming party on Saturday. Told me to invite you and said you could bring Milo too."

"How does he know about Milo?"

"Well, he said you could bring a friend," Samantha said. "I figured Milo was the obvious choice, but if you think that'll send mixed messages, then maybe not."

"I'm working the morning of Halloween, so I'll be off from work on Saturday. But I'm not sure I'm up for a party. Eli is—"

"Obnoxious at times, yes," Samantha said. "Which is more reason why I need both you and Steven there as buffers."

"Okay, I'll go."

"That took a lot of convincing."

Kathy smiled. "When have I ever turned down a party? What I need to think about is whether I'm going to invite Milo."

"You do that." Samantha stood. "I need to get back to planning my *big day*."

CHAPTER 8

Ian parked Eli Harding's car on Lookout Drive and watched as the witch's boyfriend pulled into the driveway of a Cape Cod cottage. The street was virtually treeless—to allow the homes to have a view of the lake, but the large condominium complex they were building across the street hampered that view.

As the young man walked up the driveway to the front door, he looked down at the keys in his hand, oblivious to Ian watching him.

The setting sun necessitated that he turn on the lights inside, which made it easier for Ian to peer into the windows and observe. Taking note of habits and behaviors was important to convincing people that everything was the same. Luckily, it was a skill he had been mastering for the last six years.

On a notepad, Ian wrote down 5:00 as the boyfriend's home arrival time. He had followed him in to work earlier that morning, noting that he left the house at 8:20 and arrived at work—at Erie City Hall, specifically in the Public Works department—at 8:26.

It was only a mile and a half away from his house and very easily walkable, but the boyfriend was part of Generation X and fully ingrained in car culture. Why would he walk when he could drive?

Among the other notes on his list were what the boyfriend usually wore to work—navy blue work pants and a light blue button-up—what he wore casually—jeans with a tucked-in T-shirt and leather jacket—and who he usually talked to on a daily basis—he only waved at one neighbor, was dating the witch, and was good friends with two guys from his department. Not that Ian thought he'd ever need to go to work for the boyfriend, but it was important to know, just in case.

When the light on the second floor clicked on, Ian took advantage of the growing darkness and approached the house. The trick was to walk with a purpose, as if he had every right to be where he was.

Up on the porch, Ian peered through the window. The furnishings inside weren't too bad. The couch was worn and the dining table was small and nicked—clearly a hand-me-down—but the walls held picture frames containing family photos, photo collages, and even the basic landscape images you could buy at Ames or Hills. Not bad for a bachelor pad.

Ian noted the boyfriend coming down the stairs in black jeans and a gray T-shirt under a plaid flannel—his "going out" attire. Immediately, Ian pulled away from the window and retreated to the sidewalk.

He walked casually, keeping his eye on the inside of the house. Once he got to the street corner, he turned around and went back in the opposite direction, again scoping out the inside of the house as best he could.

The boyfriend snatched up his keys on the kitchen counter and then emerged from the front door, locking it behind him. On his way to the driveway, he waved at Ian and offered a, "Hey, how are you?" before walking up the driveway to his car.

Ian returned to his own car and got behind the wheel, watching as the boyfriend backed out onto the street and turned onto Cascade Street. Ian started the car, put it in gear, and followed.

CHAPTER 9

Kathy's bed was a mess. Papers and books were spread around her and her back ached from hunching all day. She'd been working on her homework since she got home last night, only taking a break to sleep, have breakfast, go for a quick run to help her relax—it didn't work—and take a shower before jumping back into her pile of homework.

She spent most of the day struggling with her Spanish homework, referring to her Spanish-English dictionary with nearly every word to decode several sentences. The hardest part of that was then creating a response to those questions. She knew she messed up the grammar and the verbs were probably in the wrong place, but after staring at it for four hours, she just wanted it off her plate. Bilingual was something she would never be.

Instead, she had focused on the language she did know and opened up *The Age of Innocence* by Edith Wharton. It took her the next couple hours to finish the book, but she didn't mind. It gave her an excuse to lay back and relax.

Now, however, she was hunched over her notebook, jotting down the thoughts and ideas that she got from the reading. She would have to share her thoughts during the next class discussion. She liked to be prepared and have several talking points for whatever way the discussion went.

As Kathy scribbled in her notebook, she jumped when she heard the doorbell ring, the pencil tip cracking on the page when she jolted.

"Damn," she muttered and arched forward to try to look out the window. Not that she could see anything. Even if she was standing right next to the window, she'd have a hard time getting a glimpse at whoever was at the front door.

The doorbell rang again and she groaned as she stuck the notebook between the pages of *The Age of Innocence* to hold her place. Careful not to disrupt her papers, Kathy climbed out of bed and felt her spine pop all the way up her back as she finally stretched her aching muscles.

Downstairs, when she answered the door she was immediately hit with the memory of her conversation last night at dinner.

"Milo!"

"Hey." He glanced down at her at her outfit—sweatpants and a sweater. "I take it you forgot."

Kathy looked herself over as well. "I didn't forget," she lied. "You're just earlier than I thought."

"Oh, sorry. Traffic wasn't that bad."

"Milo, listen, about tonight—"

He shook his head. "You don't have to change your clothes if you don't want. Really, it's going to be very laid-back. We're just going to go back to my place, make some dinner, maybe watch a movie. Just hang out."

She thought of the two textbook chapters she still needed to read by tomorrow morning, but the happy look on his face was hard to turn down. The date Milo had planned seemed fun. And the reading could wait. She knew from experience that Friday's class discussion always took the whole class. They wouldn't start on the next chapters in the textbook until Monday.

"That sounds fun," she told him. "Let me just run up and change and I'll be ready."

"Are you sure?"

She looked down at herself again. "Yeah, I'm not one of those people who is okay with leaving the house in sweats." She laughed. "If I started now, the next thing you'd know, I wouldn't be feeding the meter or smiling to people on the sidewalk. People would riot, it'd get bad."

He laughed. "We wouldn't want that." He leaned down to

kiss her, but reflexively, she turned her head and it landed on her cheek.

In an effort to make a recovery, Kathy smiled at him and tried her best to look excited. "Let me just get changed!"

On her way up the stairs, she wondered if she was being a horrible person by going on these dates to see if she liked him. Wasn't that just leading him on? But how else would she know how she felt?

CHAPTER 10

- JULY 1983 -
ROCHESTER, NY

Ian was hopeful as he sat in the examination room waiting for Dr. Kendrick's arrival. It had been a year since the fire that had changed his life. A year since everything he had once taken for granted was ripped away from him.

Taking a warm shower.

Going outside without covering up.

Being able to go more than twenty minutes without sipping on water.

Not having a whole pharmacy of medications to take to prevent infection.

Not having people stare and whisper when he went out in public.

The list went on and on, but he was optimistic that Dr.

Kendrick would have a solution that would help bring back a semblance of his old life.

As Ian sat on the paper-lined table, he felt a sudden chill from the air conditioning blowing from the vent. It was harder now to determine the room's temperature. The fire had caused extensive nerve damage, which meant that sometimes he was sitting in a room for a while before he could tell whether he was warm or cold. That was especially dangerous in the summer months, which they were in the midst of.

The door suddenly opened and Dr. Kendrick's voice boomed as he looked over Ian's chart. "Mr. Coffed, how are you today?"

"Nervous," Ian said quietly. That had been another effect of his burns: his voice didn't quite sound like his own. He didn't know whether it was the smoke inhalation or damaged muscles beneath the thin skin on his neck. Either way, it didn't help him from assuring people his appearance shouldn't be feared.

It was hard not to be depressed when the very glimpse at a child could make them cry and run away.

"I'll bet," Dr. Kendrick said.

"Please tell me you have good news for me."

"Well, I think it's important to be realistic here. We've talked about how regaining your old way of life is incredibly unlikely." He looked over the top of the clipboard at Ian. "You're still going to that therapist I recommended you to, right?"

Ian nodded, even though he had only gone a handful of

times. All of the doctors on his team—because simply living his life now required a *team* of medical professionals—were concerned about his mental health and the toll his appearance was taking on it. Their advice was a hard pill to swallow when Ian knew his therapist generally liked the image she saw in the mirror every time. She didn't know—nor did anyone else on his *team*—exactly what he was going through.

"So what are you saying, Doc?"

Kendrick sighed heavily and then set the clipboard down on the small counter near the sink. "We've tried skin grafts, we've tried nerve transplants, we've tried a number of other remedies." He shook his head and looked to the floor.

Ian glared at him, trying to force the doctor to look him in the eyes as he delivered the news he was about to doll out.

"I'm afraid we've done all we can do."

"That's not good enough."

Dr. Kendrick's shoulders slumped. "I understand this can be hard to accept. I think another session with—"

"I don't need a shrink!" Ian erupted in his squeaky voice. "I need answers and solutions! How are you going to fix me?"

"I'm afraid I can't."

"This is the best facility in the city and you're telling me you're giving up? How am I supposed to live my life?"

"You've managed for the last year," Dr. Kendrick said calmly. "You'll adjust to this new way of life. Think of it this way: you're lucky you survived that fire. If the firemen had been a few minutes later, the whole house would've collapsed and you and I wouldn't be having this conversation right now."

Yeah, and what kind of life is this? Ian thought to himself.

"Find me another specialist," he said. "There has to be one somewhere. Cleveland, New York, Chicago, somewhere. Where's the best burn unit in the country? Better yet, the world?"

Still calm, Dr. Kendrick offered another sympathic sigh. "You could try a second opinion, but my belief is they're going to tell you more or less the same thing. Your skin has been severely damaged. Beyond repair. I sympathize with your disfigurement, but we've done all we can do."

Ian shook his head, refusing to accept that answer. If it was the last thing he did, he was going to find a way to fix the damage that had been done to him.

CHAPTER 11

See you tomorrow," Mr. Marsden said to Samantha as he passed by her cubicle. He had a bag strapped over his shoulder. Probably stuffed with files to review at home. "One more day until the weekend!"

She smiled and waved goodbye to him. "Have a nice night."

"Don't stay too late," he said.

"I won't. I'm on my way out myself."

"Good! Wouldn't want to burn out my best worker. See you later!" He turned and stepped through the office door.

Samantha collected her purse from where it was stashed in the bottom drawer of her desk and scanned her work area for anything she might need to make a note of for tomorrow's activities. Unlike Mr. Marsden, she had a tendency to mentally leave work at the office when she went home, so if she didn't leave herself notes or to-do lists, she would forget what she wanted to do and nothing would get done each day.

"I think that's it," she murmured quietly to herself. Swiveling around, she started to rise to her feet, but the phone at her desk rang. With a sigh, she sank back down in her chair, turned and looked at the phone.

Did she dare answer it? Technically it wasn't quite five o'clock, so the office *was* open for a few more minutes.

Cursing her moral compass, she picked up the phone and answered, "Darius Wilcox, CPA, this is Samantha."

"Sam, hi, it's Steven."

It wasn't what she expected to hear on the other end. "I'm sorry?"

"The man you're going to marry…"

"Oh!" She brought a hand to her forehead and rubbed her head. "It's been a long day. Why are you calling me at the office?"

"I wanted to catch you before you left," he said. "I scheduled a time tomorrow for cake testing. Right after work at this bakery downtown."

"Tomorrow? I didn't realize you were going to schedule that."

"I don't think we can put off these wedding plans anymore if you want to get married in January," he said. "You don't have anything going on tomorrow, do you?"

"Well, I'm getting paid tomorrow so I thought I'd go grocery shopping after work." She made a mental note to add more candy for trick-or-treaters to the list. She wasn't sure if she had enough. Last year they were completely wiped out by 7:00.

"Oh, sorry. You could go shopping Saturday morning."

"I guess," she said with a sigh. There would only be slim pickings of candy Saturday morning. "Did the bakery not have any other openings?"

"Well…"

"Steven," she said as a warning, because she suspected that she wasn't going to like what he was about to say.

"Tomorrow was the best day for my mom and ever since we met yesterday, she's been hounding me to make an appointment."

"So you made sure your *mother* could come but not your *bride*?"

"Well, when you put it like that…"

"How else am I supposed to put it?" she nearly shouted and quickly lowered her voice into an angry whisper. "You and I are the ones getting married, which means you and *I* need to be making these decisions *together*. Your mother is a very distant second. Maybe even third! Hell, I think Kathy would come before your mother."

"Because she's *your* family?" he asked.

"That's not what this is about."

"Sounds like it to me."

"Kathy's not trying to plan this wedding for us."

"And neither is my mother."

Samantha stopped herself from responding further. Arguing over the phone while she was still at work was not what she wanted to do. Arguing at all was what she had been trying to avoid by having a small wedding.

"Where and when are we meeting tomorrow?" she asked.

"Mighty Fine Bakery on State and 4th. Be there by 5:30."

Samantha scribbled out the details on a scrap piece of paper. "Okay, I'll be there."

"'Kay," he said, then hung up without a goodbye.

CHAPTER 12

Kathy laughed as Milo danced to George Michaels' "Faith" while he sprinkled cheese on the pizza. Only a small portion actually made it on the pie, the rest scattered all over the counter, and some even fell to the floor.

It was nice to see him acting different than he usually did. He was fun, carefree, unashamed of looking goofy. That helped Kathy relax and she danced along to the music as well, although not nearly as intense as Milo did. He was clearly trying to impress her, which would ordinarily make her hesitate but for the moment, she indulged because she liked being around him.

Milo attempted to scoop some of the cheese from the counter back onto the pizza, but he refused to stop shaking his hips and bopping his head, which resulted in not much getting back to the dish. Kathy laughed again and when the song ended, he finally paused the dance party long enough to lay an even amount of cheese.

Michael Jackson began singing "The Way You Make Me Feel" and Milo joined in, singing off-key and trying his best to mimic the dance moves. Kathy smiled and nudged him away.

"Careful, before you break something," she said with a laugh.

Milo only took half a step backward and continued to dance, moving in close as Kathy stepped forward to finish putting the toppings on the pizza.

As he serenaded her, Kathy admitted to herself that she had been wrong. This morning, she had been dreading coming here, afraid she was leading him on. But now that she was here, she realized she was having fun. There was absolutely no pressure and it was good to laugh again. It'd been a while since she had.

Kathy put their dinner in the oven, set the timer, and took part in another one of Milo's dance breaks with him. It was what the two of them knew together, having met during a night out on the town. Forgetting the mess, they both moved to the music as if they were back at the 814 Nightclub and not in Milo's kitchen.

When the timer buzzed, they were both pulled away from their fantasy. Kathy moved to check on the food. Milo fanned his shirt.

"I'm hot."

"You think it might've had anything to do with those slick moves?" she asked.

"Are they working?" he asked, with a flicker of his eyebrows.

"Don't get ahead of yourself," she said. "Pizza's done." She pulled it out and set it on the stovetop, fanning it with the oven mitts to try to cool it off faster.

"Good. I'm starving." He turned off the radio. "Been working up an appetite. You mind if I crack open a window?"

Kathy looked out into the darkness and wondered if it was still raining. It had started when they first got to Milo's and they had to run inside.

"No, go ahead," she told him. "It is a little stuffy in here."

As he crossed the room to open the window by the dining table, Kathy used the pizza cutter and dished out a couple slices on two plates and brought them over.

They both sat down to eat. Milo looked at her as she took her first bite. "So how'd I do?"

Kathy raised an eyebrow and pointed down to her plate with her free hand. "Um, I helped make this too. Actually, I probably made most of it. You were too busy playing back-up dancer to America's Top 40 artists."

He smiled. "True. But I meant the date in general. Are you relaxed? That was my goal."

She smirked and shrugged, playing coy. "We'll have to see. The only thing you've done so far is put me to work."

Milo laughed. "Ouch. Okay. I guess that's fair." He reached

out for her hand. "I like being with you, Kathy."

She squeezed his hand back and held it there. "I like being with you too."

Kathy watched as he took a bite—clumsily because he only had one free hand—and she thought that maybe someday she could like him like she liked other guys in the past. Her problem must be everything else in her life making her run around in circles. School and work and thinking about Samantha's wedding was having ripple effects into the rest of her life. She needed to start enjoying each moment. Like this one.

When they finished eating, Kathy looked over at the kitchen.

"And now back to reality," she said.

"Leave it, I can clean it up later."

"I'm not going to leave your house a mess," she said. "It'll get done faster with the two of us. I'll wash and you dry. Deal?"

"Sounds good to me," he said.

They carried their dishes back to the kitchen and Kathy began filling the sink with soapy water. One-by-one, Milo added a pile of dirty dishes to the counter beside the sink as he cleaned the rest of the kitchen.

When he was done cleaning up his mess, Milo stood behind her and started rubbing her shoulders.

Kathy shrugged him off. "Can you start drying these?" she asked. "I'm running out of room to put them."

"Sure thing." His hand lingered on her back as he stepped

around her and grabbed a dish towel to start drying.

Between each one, he found an excuse to touch her. Kissing her shoulder, touching her back as he moved around her, trying to rub her shoulders again. At one point, while moving to the other side of the sink—again—he leaned over and hugged her from behind.

"Milo, that's enough," she told him.

"What?" he asked.

"That's making me a little uncomfortable."

He sighed heavily. "Sorry."

From his tone, she could tell that something else was bothering him, but she didn't want to bring it up while she was still working at the dishes. She looked down and saw that she only had one more. Finishing it up, she set it to the side, and cleaned up the sink.

As Milo put away the final dish, she dried her hands and leaned back against the counter in Milo's direction.

"What's the matter?" she asked.

"Nothing."

"If you're not going to tell me, there's no way we can fix the problem."

"I wasn't aware we were able to fix something that isn't there." He leaned against the counter on the other side of the kitchen.

She narrowed her eyes. "What are you talking about? You're the one who couldn't keep your hands off me."

"And you wouldn't let me."

"That makes me a bad person?" she asked.

"No," he said through another sigh. "Of course it doesn't. It's just…frustrating."

"Is this because I won't sleep with you?" she asked.

"No," he said. "Not exactly. But also, you're not giving me *anything*."

"We held hands at dinner."

"And other than a few cheek kisses here and there, that's all we do," he said. "We don't hold hands, we only see each other once or twice a week. I mean, come on, Kathy. Are we dating or are we just friends? I'm okay with either, but I need to know."

As a distraction, Kathy said, "We've been dating for two months now."

"We've gone on dates, sure, but you're usually not present at them," he said. "You seem to be watching the clock until it's over or not paying attention to what I'm saying."

"I've been a little busy lately," she said. "I'm sorry I'm not doting over you."

"I know you have a lot going on," he said. "But when I'm with you, I'm with *you*. Not everything else in my life. I don't think it's unfair to expect the same in return."

Kathy crossed her arms and looked away. He had a point. And this was exactly what Samantha had warned her about.

"Tonight was fun," he added. "I feel like we really connected—until we didn't. I don't know if you started thinking about everything else and changed your mind about us, or maybe it's something else entirely. But I need you to answer this: do you even want to be with me?"

Kathy stared down at the floor, contemplating what to say, but nothing came to mind. In the meantime, Milo's question lay unanswered and heavy in the silence between them, which said more than words ever could.

Finally, Milo shook his head and stepped away from her.

CHAPTER 13

Ian sat in Eli's car and watched from the street as the boyfriend arrived home. He pulled in the driveway, parked back near the garage, and walked up to the front door with his keys in one hand and a briefcase in the other. He had a pensive look and seemed otherwise oblivious to his surroundings.

Typical.

In Ian's experience, most people paid no attention to the world around them. Too consumed in their selfish thoughts; their own lives. It was only getting worse. But Ian was going to take full advantage of that.

In the car, he pulled out the bottle of chloroform and doused a rag with it, letting the excess spill on the floor of the car between his legs. He continued to watch the boyfriend while he recapped the bottle and slipped the rag in his back pocket.

The boyfriend stepped through the front door, clicked on the lights in the living room, and then set his briefcase on the kitchen counter. Ian watched what little he could from across the street. He'd been sitting there a while and several wet leaves fell on the windshield, further concealing the car.

It was one of the reasons fall and winter were Ian's two favorite seasons. Both cold and dreary, giving people even more reason to worry only about what was going on inside their homes and not what was happening to their neighbors.

Another reason was that the day ended sooner in these seasons. Darkness was always welcome when finding new skin. As was isolation, which these seasons also encouraged.

Through the window, Ian watched as the boyfriend escaped to the back bedroom. Likely to change out of his work clothes. Now was the time to act.

Stepping out of the car, again walking with a purpose to cast off any wandering glances, Ian stepped onto the porch and through the front door as if he was visiting an old friend. The boyfriend had left the front door unlocked—what a foolish thing to do for someone dating a witch. Ian closed the door quietly behind him and locked it.

This place was dingier than he thought. Certainly didn't look as nice as the outside of the house did from the street. He noted the briefcase sitting on the kitchen counter, surrounded by stacks of newspapers, magazines, and mail. He expected the place to be tidier.

But Ian wasn't here to admire decor. He moved through the house, his wet shoes squeaking on the old hardwood. Noting the noise, he moved quick.

The boyfriend peeked his head out of the door with his shirt half unbuttoned.

"Eli? What are you—" His eyes grew large when he saw Ian's face curled into a sinister grin. He darted back into the room, but the intruder was faster.

The boyfriend attempted to shut himself in the bedroom, but Ian slammed his hand against the cheap builder-grade door and forced it open. He pounced, knocking his target to the floor where they struggled.

The boyfriend swung punches and squirmed to get out from under Ian. But Ian was strong—or rather, Eli Harding was.

"What are you doing?" the boyfriend asked. "Get off me!"

Ian smiled. The boyfriend still thought he was the witch's neighbor. Behind him, Ian fished for the rag in his back pocket, struggling to hold the boyfriend in place.

Only having one hand on him gave the boyfriend opportunity. He threw his head back, slamming into Ian's nose, breaking it. The injury wouldn't last, but the pain was certainly present.

The boyfriend got to his feet and ran out of the bedroom. Ian followed, blood running down his face and soaking his T-shirt. He'd have to get more clothes from Eli's house if he wanted to use this skin again.

Ian ran after the boyfriend, who was caught up by the locked front door, and tackled him in the small hallway by the entry. They crashed to the floor again, but Ian was better prepared this time. He had the rag in his hand and brought it to the boyfriend's face, covering his mouth and nose.

The boyfriend squirmed, trying to hold his breath and wriggle himself free from under Ian's weight. The struggle lasted a while, but finally, nature gave in and he was forced to take a breath and breathe in the chemicals. Shortly after, he stopped moving and went limp on the floor.

Ian stood and watched the boyfriend for a moment to make certain he wasn't somehow faking it. When he was sure the boyfriend wouldn't move, Ian went back to the bedroom and rifled through the dresser, pulling out a complete change of clothes.

Once his own blood-soaked clothes were removed, Ian began peeling at his flesh, ripping pieces off his body and tossing them in a pile in the corner, as if it were laundry. Slowly, Ian removed every trace of Eli Harding's appearance until all that was left was the true appearance of Ian—a mottled, distorted semblance of something that might be human, distorted through years of changing his appearance.

The switch to his true form didn't last long, though. Shortly after, Ian's scarred body began twitching. His skin began to bubble up, sprouting hair, a different skin tone, and hair color he had never had before. Within minutes, Ian's body had morphed from Eli Harding into the boyfriend.

Ian pulled on the clothes from the dresser, looked in the mirror, and smiled.

The next phase of his plan was about to begin. But first he needed to take care of the boyfriend.

CHAPTER 14

Kathy slammed the front door as she stormed into the house.

"Excuse me!" Samantha called from the kitchen. "In this house, only one witch can stew at a time!"

The younger sister walked back to the kitchen, where Samantha was stirring something in a pot on the stove. From the foul smell, she guessed it was a potion.

"I just had to take the bus home because I couldn't stand to be with Milo for another minute!" Kathy said.

"So I take it you two are over?"

"No. Maybe. I don't know."

"So I guess you haven't figured out your feelings for him." Samantha sprinkled another ingredient into the pot and waved away the fumes with a disgusted face. "By the way, remind me to light a candle when I'm done with this. It smells terrible."

"What are you making?" Kathy asked.

"A truth potion." Samantha knocked the wooden spoon on the edge of the pot and set it on the spoon rest. "Refilling our stock. But you're not off the hook with your Milo story. Spill. What happened?"

Kathy sighed and rolled her eyes. "You were right."

Samantha pulled up her ear. "I'm sorry, what was that? Could you repeat it?"

Kathy shot her sister a look. "You heard me."

"I know, but I just wanted to hear it again. So what happened?"

"We went back to his place, made dinner, danced. It was a lot of fun. But when we were cleaning up, he was being flirty and a little handsy. I told him to back off, and he did, but it brought up a whole argument about whether we're actually dating."

Samantha reached for the spoon again and stirred the potion. "Because you wouldn't let him touch you?"

"Because I *never* let him touch me," Kathy clarified. "He asked me point-blank if I even wanted to be with him."

"What did you say?"

Kathy shrugged. "I didn't say anything."

"Oooh." Samantha dragged out the vowel. "Obviously he didn't like that."

"I mean, he was disappointed, but he said he wasn't going to hold it against me."

"Well, if you're going to shift to just being friends, give it some time for emotions to cool down."

"That's the thing, I'm not sure that I *want* to shift to just being friends." That got her a stern look. "Kathy, you can't keep stringing this poor guy along. You have to decide: do you want to be with him or not?"

"I know! I need to make a decision. That's why I left on my own. I didn't want him to feel obligated to take me home. We both need space to think about…everything. I just feel like there's something wrong with me."

"In what way?"

"Lately I haven't been interested in dating anyone."

Samantha fell back against the cabinets in exaggerated shock. "Stop the presses! Kathy Walker is taking herself *off the market*?"

Kathy rolled her eyes again and smirked. "Ha. Ha. No, I mean, Milo is awesome, but I'm not feeling any sparks between us. And trust me, I keep trying. But I think that's just hurting him more."

"Letting him hold your hand or kiss you or something might help you decide," Samantha said. "If you don't feel anything, then there's your answer."

"I know. We did have something when we first met. Or, I *thought* we did. But now it just feels…uncomfortable. Like it's forced, you know? I've never had this problem before."

"So maybe you and Milo just aren't meant to be. You had some chemistry before, but sometimes there just isn't anything more than that."

"Well, I feel the same way about the guy in my English class that asked me out yesterday."

Samantha scoffed. "Of course you'd have no shortage of men vying for your attention. Even when you're giving off uninterested signals. What was wrong with this guy?"

"He just seemed, I don't know, *juvenile*."

"Well, it is an entry-level college class," Samantha said. "They're—what?—eighteen- and nineteen-year-olds? You're twenty-one. Those two or three years make a difference."

"Maybe."

"Look, Kathy, I think you're just being pickier with the guys you date. That's not a bad thing. You were with Jeremy for a while and you matured a lot from that relationship. You learned more about yourself and what you need from the guys you date. Plus, you're changing. You're going to school now and you're working. Every day, you're bettering yourself. Obviously your standards for the men in your life are changing too. So take some time to worry about yourself and don't pay attention to any guys until there *is* that spark."

Kathy grinned. "Yeah, you're probably right. But guys are usually so fun, though."

Samantha rolled her eyes and stirred the contents of the pot again with the wooden spoon. "Guess there's still a bit of immaturity left in you."

Kathy's jaw dropped and her cheeks turned up in a grin. "And let's talk about you, Little Miss Judgement!"

"Soon to be *missus*," Samantha added.

"Is that what's going on with the truth potion?" Kathy asked. "Does it have anything to do with why you're stewing? Wedding plans gone awry?"

"Well, I thought I'd restock our truth potions because Steven keeps withholding the truth from me."

Kathy's eyes grew large. "He's lying to you? Is he having an affair? Did you find out from your new power? I thought you weren't brain-picking people?" The questions came out in a single breath, one right after the other.

"No, he's not cheating. And no, I'm not using my telepathic abilities on any nonmagical people, although it would certainly help me get a better feel for what Steven's mother thinks of me since it's obvious she's not going to back off anytime soon."

"Oh, this is a mother-in-law thing. Both of you are trying to claim ownership over the same person."

"He's not my *property*," Samantha said.

"No, but he's your boo."

"My what?"

"Your honey. Your sweetie. Your *shnookums*."

Samantha laughed. "I've never called him *that*."

"You get the point. So what's the deal with Mama Harper?"

"Oh, it's petty in the grand scheme of things." Samantha

turned back to the potion and turned off the gas on the stove. "I feel like he's planning this wedding with her and not with me."

"Which parts have the two of them decided on without you?" Kathy asked.

"What do you mean?"

"Well, you and I started shopping for your dress—which you still need to decide on, by the way—and you and Steven both decided on the caterer and the photographer—"

"But not before *she* made sure we knew her disapproval of all of those choices," Samantha cut in. "And yesterday she was talking about changing the venue too!"

"Regardless of what she *says*, you and Steven still made all of the final decisions together," Kathy pushed.

"Well, Steven invited her to the cake tasting tomorrow. Which, by the way, I'm going to need my car to go to so you're going to have to take the bus to school."

Kathy nodded. "Fine, I suppose the bus is okay."

"Since you're borrowing *my* car, you really don't have a choice."

"Let's not change the subject. We're still talking about your grudge against Steven's mom."

"It's not a grudge! I'm just tired of her being a constant presence in all of this wedding planning."

"Sam, she's his mother. Your future mother-in-law. She's not going away. This is a big moment in her son's life, of course she's going to be a part of it. You need to learn to work with her because in the grand scheme of things, the relationship that you have with Steven is easier to replace than the one he has with his mother. Don't put him in the middle of it where he has to make a choice between you and her. He loves you both."

Samantha took a deep breath as she swallowed that pill. Admitting defeat wasn't her strong suit. But Kathy was right, she needed to take the high road with Mary for the sake of her relationship with Steven. It would make it easier for everyone if the two of them got along.

"So it seems we've both been acting a bit immature," Samantha muttered.

"Um, I would say you more than me," Kathy said with a smirk. "I'm not the one fixing up a potion or putting Milo under a spell. You took it to the next level of crazy."

Samantha laughed. "Steven's marrying a witch, so he should know I'm at least a little crazy."

CHAPTER 15

- JULY 1983 -
ROCHESTER, NY

Ian pulled the hoodie tight to his face as he waited for the bus. Between his long time in the hospital, his frequent trips to doctors appointments—which all came with bills—and his appearance unable to get him a job, he was near broke. The only thing saving him was unemployment, as pitifully low as that was. He had enough to pay for his tiny, crappy apartment, some food, and public transportation, but not much else.

As he waited, he felt sweat begin to trickle from the few parts of his skin that hadn't been as badly damaged. The few areas that still had pores, which really equated to the parts that had been covered that night of the fire. Not much, since it had been just as hot that night and he had been asleep.

With the arrival of sweat, he knew that a bath was in his

future. Any amount of dirt on his irritated skin would cause infection, which could be deadly. All things the doctors on his *team* would never have to deal with.

A part of him wanted to set fire to the houses of each of his doctors, hoping for a similar outcome. But his appearance would give him away. Not to mention, running—and moving in general—was difficult due to chaffing. He spent forever each night trying to get comfortable on the couch or in bed, only to have to readjust twenty minutes later.

Arson was off the table. He would have to find another way to get revenge on his doctors.

By time Ian made it back to his apartment just north of downtown, the sweat was making his skin itch. It took all of his willpower not to scrape the remaining appendages on his hand—the remnants of his fingers—over his smooth and worn skin. He had tried that once, only to erupt in excruciating pain.

A cool bath was the only solution.

In the bathroom, he ran the water and slowly undressed, careful not to drag his clothes over his skin, causing unexpected scrapes or sores.

The bathroom was small. He had to maneuver around the toilet to start the water for the tub. On the opposite wall of the tub was the counter with a wide mirror.

All the better to hate what I see in it, he thought to himself every time he saw it.

However, now that he was undressed, he forced himself to

look in the mirror. Really take a good, hard look at himself. There was virtually no hair, other than the few tufts on his head, which he cut back every few weeks or so when it got unruly. His right eye was nearly scarred shut and the eyelid of his left eye moved laboriously. That had been several surgeries in itself.

At first glance, he looked nearly emaciated. Skin and bones, as they called it. But that skin was shiny, as if it was plastic-wrap stretched nearly to its breaking point.

His arms showed scars of failed skin grafts, which only got worse the further down he looked. He had two fingers and a thumb left on his right arm and three fingers and a thumb on his left. His signature had been reduced to an X and he had purchased several of those claw-things the elderly used so they didn't need to bend over to pick up things. Only, Ian needed it for everyday functions.

This was it. This was who he had become. Reduced to someone the world wanted to forget. To stash away in the bad part of town and never associate with. And this was who he would continue to be. All the hope he had allowed himself to have, the faith he had in his *team*, was ripped away from him nearly as quickly as the fire had taken everything else from him.

In a sudden burst of anger, Ian threw his fists at the mirror, sending cracks like spiderwebs all over it. He smashed it again and again, shards falling to the floor, digging into his damaged skin. His rage masked any immediate pain.

Finally, he sunk to the tiled floor—brown from hard water

and rusty pipes—and saw that he was bleeding.

The thought hadn't occurred to him. Of course he could still bleed. And even though most of his nerves were damaged, he still felt things, even if all it was was depression.

In that moment, Ian knew that he was still human. Still living. Even if the way he was didn't seem like a life worth living.

CHAPTER 16

Kathy followed the other students into the classroom for her English class. Everyone had the same listless expression that came with morning classes. Like zombies, they all filed in and took their usual seats.

As the room filled and Roger stepped through the door, Kathy took notice at who *wasn't* there: Harry. He usually sat two seats down from her and would partner up with her for group discussions.

And apparently the whole time he was pining after her.

Is that why he's not here? she wondered, then decided that was beyond conceited. There was definitely more going on in Harry's life than his crush on the girl who sat next to him in class.

When the clock hit 8:00 on the dot, Roger said hello to the class and dove into the day's activities, which consisted of a few housekeeping items—textbook readings and reflections were due on Monday—before he started off the class discussion of Edith Wharton's book.

At the end of the hour after the class was over and the rest of the students were exiting the room, Roger walked up to Kathy and pointed to Harry's empty seat.

"Have you talked to him? Is he sick?"

Kathy glanced over at the empty chair and shrugged. "I guess so. I haven't heard from him since Wednesday." *When I completely brushed him off instead of giving him a proper answer.*

"Okay. I'll have to put together work for him," he said. "I know it's college, but I cut some slack for these one-oh-one classes." He turned back to his papers spread out on the podium.

Kathy stepped to the front of the room. "If you want, I can drop off the work to Harry myself. That way, he can get a few extra days head-start on it and you don't have to announce to the rest of the class that you take it easy on us when he comes back."

Roger smiled at her. "I would like to keep that my little secret. Are you sure you wouldn't mind?"

It'll give me an excuse to check on Harry and properly apologize. "Not at all," she said.

He rifled through his collection of papers and put together a stack. On a scrap piece of paper, he scribbled out Harry's address and added it to the top of the small pile.

"Thank you," he said. "It isn't much, so it won't take him too long. Since he missed today's discussion, I want him to do a two-page reflection on the reading in addition to the one that's due Monday. His address is on top. If he has any questions, my number is in the syllabus."

Kathy took the stack from him and nodded. "I'll relay the message."

"Thanks for this," he said. "I really appreciate it and I'm sure Harry will too."

"No problem." She offered a wave as she walked out of the room.

She pressed Harry's stack against her chest once she got outside in the wind. It was gloomy, even a bit misty. The damp air sent a chill right through her, but it only made her think of how cozy and warm her house would be. Maybe she'd light a fire in the fireplace in the living room and do her homework there before Samantha got home. She could even make some tea and put on a nice warm sweater to help warm her up and—

"Kathy!"

She pulled herself out of her head at the sound of her name and looked around the vast parking lot. The large expanse of pavement only made the wind worse.

Finally, her eyes landed on Milo.

"I take it you're no longer mad at me?" she said as she walked over to him.

"Yeah, about that…I wanted to apologize for putting you on the spot."

"You didn't do anything wrong," she said. "You had every right to tell me how you feel. I was the one holding back."

Milo shook his head. "And I was trying to force a response out of you. We were both at fault. Anyway, that's not what I came here to talk about and it's not where I wanted last night to go, either. I asked you to my house so you could relax, not to cause you even more drama."

Kathy smirked. "It's okay. I appreciate you trying. I should actually be the one apologizing to you. I've been sending you mixed messages and I need to stop. It's not fair to you." She motioned to the building behind her. "My life is just changing a lot and I'm not sure where you fit in to it all. But don't stop trying to fit in somewhere. Eventually, I'm sure it'll click."

He smiled.

"Aren't you supposed to be at work right now?"

"I took the day off to do things outside around the house and it doesn't look like the weather's going to hold up." He nodded back to his car. "Why don't you hop in and I'll take you home? I know you probably have a lot of homework, so I won't stay, but you'll get home faster with me than the bus."

Kathy looked down at Milo's papers pressed against her. "Well, I have to make a pitstop on my way home…"

He shrugged and went around to the passenger door and held it open for her. "So we'll stop on the way. I don't mind."

SHAPESHIFTER

Kathy tried to think of a way out of what would be a terribly awkward situation, but couldn't come up with one that wouldn't hurt Milo more than she already had. So instead, she offered him a smile, came around the car, and got in the passenger seat.

CHAPTER 17

Discomfort brought Steven back to consciousness. His head was pounding, his wrists ached, and his back and shoulder muscles burned from his arms being lifted above his head for so long.

When he opened his eyes, he didn't immediately recognize where he was. It was dark. And it smelled musty. But mostly, his mind was focused on the pain he felt.

Looking up, he saw his wrists were tied tightly together with rope that was wrapped around one of the wooden rafters above him. That explained the discomfort. He tried to wiggle his hands free—or, at the very least, loosen the binds—but the movement only served to irritate his skin further.

Instead, Steven resigned himself to look around to get a

better idea of where he was. Above him, intermixed between the beams was piping and wiring that snaked around the space. In the corner he noticed a crude-looking wooden staircase and two small windows near the top of the wall at the opposite end.

A basement. But whose was it?

Beside him, Steven noticed someone else hanging in the same way he was tied up. He looked younger, maybe late-teens, and Steven feared he was dead. His head hung forward, his chin resting on his chest.

Swinging his leg—which was still in the dress pants he wore to the office—Steven reached toward the kid and nudged him with his toes. That was when he noticed his shoes were gone—but maybe he took them off when he got home from the office. *Did* he make it home? His brain was still fuzzy.

"Hey," he croaked with a dry voice. "Are you awake?"

The kid stirred, which gave Steven some relief.

Steven nudged him again and the kid picked his head up. "Huh?"

"Are you okay?" His heart raced the longer he spent here—the more his brain had time to wrap around the fact that he was *stuck* here—but he tried to keep his voice steady and not show his panic.

"Tired," the boy said softly. "Hungry."

"Me too," Steven admitted. "Do you have any idea where we are?"

The boy grunted. "Some psycho's house."

Steven had surmised that much.

The kid nodded to two white boxes at the end of the room. One tall, the other short and wide. "There are bodies in there."

"*Bodies?*" A flicker of fear slipped into his voice. His eyes finally focused on the boxes and he saw that there were freezers.

"Yeah. Two of them. He said I'd end up in there if I screamed or tried to escape."

"How long have you been in here?"

"I don't know. A while. Probably a couple days."

"A couple days? You haven't eaten in a *couple days*?"

The boy shook his head slightly. "No. He comes down once a day, force-feeds me something dry and bland. If I don't eat it all at once then I go hungry."

"What about water?" Steven asked.

"He gives me one bottle a day. All at once, though."

Steven couldn't imagine what the boy must've gone through. And what Steven was about to go through himself. Surely, this was the type of thing Samantha battled with Kathy. She would catch on that he was missing. He and the boy just needed to hold out long enough until the sisters could get them out of here.

Upstairs, they heard footsteps and soft singing. As if the nice, normal, happy world was only at the top of the staircase, completely separate from the nightmare going on down here.

"Hey!" Steven shouted. "Help us!"

"Stop it!" The boy sprung to life and shot a panicked look at

Steven. "That's *him*!"

Steven studied the boy's face and listened for anything coming from upstairs. The singing had stopped. His heart pounded in his chest as he waited for the sound of the basement door opening, but it never came. Instead, the footsteps carried from directly above them to further in the house.

"The only times I see him are when he comes down to feed me," the boy explained. "Except when he brought you down."

"So you've seen who he is? What he looks like?"

The boy hesitated, then said, "When he brought you down, he looked…like you."

"Like me? What are you talking about?" Steven didn't have any siblings. He did, however, have a cousin who people often mistook for his brother, but Ryan lived in North Carolina. There'd be no reason he'd be in Erie, especially not at the end of October. He only ever visited in the summer time. And, above all else, Ryan wasn't a psychopath.

"He had your face," the boy said calmly. "Weird, I know. But after he brought me here, there was one point where he looked like me too. Said he needed to borrow my face for a little bit."

"Borrow your face?" Steven stared at the boy. His face seemed perfectly intact. This was *definitely* Samantha's kind of problem.

"He must need to borrow yours for some reason too." The boy looked over at the freezers. "I just don't know what they did that made him kill them and not just tie them up."

Steven followed his stare and wondered the same thing. "Don't worry. My fiancée can help us. She'll be able to figure out something is wrong and she'll come save us."

He wondered how good this kidnapper guy was at "borrowing faces." Maybe he would put on a believable act that would even fool Samantha. Or, maybe he'd kill her before she had the chance to do anything to save him.

"I hope so," the boy said. "At least now I'll have someone to talk to."

Steven smirked, trying his best to be friendly. "Yeah. I'm Steven, by the way. What's your name?"

"Harry."

CHAPTER 18

Kathy and Milo walked up to the front steps of Harry's house on Stough Avenue, not a word between them. Kathy felt guilty for bringing Milo here, especially as he realized her "pitstop" was someone's house and not a quick trip to the grocery store.

Harry's house was a white ranch on a corner lot with a beautiful ash tree out front with yellow leaves. It was one of the few trees in the neighborhood that hadn't lost all of its leaves for the season.

When the front door swung open, a short, plump woman stood just inside the screen door. Her face was drawn and her red hair hung limply around her round face.

"Can I help you?" she asked.

Kathy smiled. "Hi, are you Harry's mom?"

The woman stared at Kathy intensely before nodding."

"Well, I'm Kathy and I'm in Harry's English class. I'm just dropping off the homework since he wasn't there today. Is he around?"

The woman turned back to the house. "Frank! Frank, come here!"

"Is there something wrong?" Milo asked.

The woman broke into tears as her husband stepped into view. He quickly wrapped his arms around her and turned to Kathy and Milo.

"Who are you?"

"I'm Kathy. I'm in Harry's English class." Her smile faded. "What's going on? Is something wrong with Harry?"

Frank looked down at his wife, then turned back to his visitors. "Harry's been, uh…missing for a couple days."

Kathy stared at him blankly. Her mind ran wild with the possibilities of where Harry could have gone. Did someone snatch him up at the college? Was it at home? At work? Did he even have a job? There was so much about him she didn't know.

The worst thought of all came to her: was he taken because of her? It wouldn't be the first time someone was a target because of who she was. But was that being selfish to think that his disappearance had anything to do with her? People disappeared—or worse—all the time without it having anything to do with magic and witches.

"I'm so sorry," Milo offered. "Have you called the police?"

Frank nodded. "Yes, of course. Right when he didn't come home on Tuesday. They've begun an investigation and we've done some searches, but…" He trailed off and shook his head, cradling his wife.

"I'm sure the police know what they're doing," Milo said. "And they're probably doing their best to find him."

Frank nodded, tears welling up in his eyes. "It's been more than forty-eight hours and the odds aren't in his favor anymore."

"I'm sorry," Milo said again. "We'll get out of your hair and let you be. Good luck with everything. Sorry to bother you." He turned and took one step down, but stopped when Kathy continued to stare at Harry's parents. "Kathy?"

"I'm confused," she finally said.

"About what?" Frank asked. His wife took notice and looked up from where she had pressed her face against her husband's chest.

"You said Harry didn't come home Tuesday? And that's the last time you saw him?"

"Yes, that's right."

"But he was in class on Wednesday."

"Are you sure?" Harry's mother asked. "Did you talk to him? Did he sound healthy? Taken-care of? Did he give any indication of where he might be staying?"

Kathy held up her hands. "That's all I know. He was in class,

I talked to him for a bit. Nothing of substance. Mostly about the class."

"Well, what did he say?" she pushed. "Did you see where he went? Do you know why he didn't come to class today? Why won't you tell me where our son is!?" Her voice grew hysterical and tears pooled over from her eyes.

"Martha, shh," Frank said. "Let's not scare away the best lead we've had so far." He looked to Kathy. "Would you mind leaving your contact information so that the police can get in touch with you for questions?"

Kathy shot a look back at Milo, who was hiding his emotions under a stoic mask. She turned back to Harry's parents and said, "Sure."

Frank disappeared deeper inside the house a moment and came back with a pad of paper and a pen.

Kathy leaned against the railing on the porch and wrote her name and phone number.

"I just don't understand," Martha said. "He had no reason to run away. He was healthy, happy. Had a good relationship with both of us, I think. Always told us where he'd be and when he'd be home. You just don't think this kind of stuff happens to you. It happens to other people far away or people on TV. I can't even—I just wish I knew where he was. That he was safe."

Kathy handed the pad of paper back to Frank. "I am so sorry that you're both going through this. I hope he comes home soon. If there's anything I can do to help, let the police know and they can get in touch with me. And you can call me directly too, but I'm afraid I've told you all I know. I really wish I knew more."

"Thank you," Martha said.

Kathy offered a sad smile and then retreated back to the car with Milo. She braced herself for the questions she knew would follow. But Milo was silent as he started the car, shifted it into gear, and pulled out of the driveway.

Once they were on the street, however, he started.

"What the *hell* was that, Kathy?"

"I know for a fact that I saw him on Wednesday," she said, her response already ready. "What was I supposed to do? Lie? This could bring back their son!"

"It was pretty low of you to bring me here after all of that talk about working things out with us," he said. "You realize you asked me to take you to some other guy's house, right? And you thought I'd just be okay with that?"

"That's not what this was." She crossed her arms and looked out the window. She was glad they were in the car where the weight of his stare wouldn't break down her defiance.

"Do you know where he is?" Milo asked. "That kid? Are you seeing him even though he's supposed to be missing? Is that how he was in class on Wednesday? Did you just slip up when you said you saw him?"

She turned her body in the car so she was facing him. "Are

you seriously asking me that? Do you think I would do that?"

Milo raised a hand off the steering wheel and made a face, as if to say, "Who knows?"

"If you even *think* that I'm capable of doing that, there is absolutely no future for us," she told him. "What reason would I have to hide him and lie to his parents about it?"

"Maybe you're sleeping with him."

"You're an incredibly selfish person, you know that? This poor guy is missing and you're more worried about yourself and the fact that you're not getting laid. Grow up."

Milo clenched his jaw, but didn't say anything else. Kathy turned back in her seat and faced forward, again crossing her arms. By the way Milo drove—running yellow lights, jerking the wheel around turns, and coming to abrupt stops—she could tell that he was mad.

Good, she thought. *Let him be. I have nothing to say to him anyway.*

When they pulled onto Kathy's street, Milo put the car in park and turned to her.

"Look, I'm sorry for what I said. It was just a surprise to go to that kid's—"

Kathy got out of the car and shut the door while Milo was mid-sentence. At the moment, she didn't want to hear another word from him. She wanted to send a message that he couldn't make those kinds of accusations of her.

She refused to look back at Milo as she walked up the

stoop to the front. The engine roared loudly when he pulled away, which told her that her message had gotten through to him.

CHAPTER 19

– SEPTEMBER 1983 –
BUFFALO, NY

Tell me good news, Doc." Ian sat nervously in the small examination room at the Erie County Medical Center in Buffalo. Not willing to accept Dr. Kendrick's diagnosis in Rochester, he decided to get a second opinion from a whole different medical group.

Dr. Bennett was accomplished, as was obvious by the various degrees and awards hanging on the wall in her waiting room. Unlike Ian's present state, she had beautiful skin that seemed to glow, framed by her long dark hair. She smelled great too, adding to her overall beauty.

She studied his chart before answering, a frown very apparent on her face. "Well, it seems that Dr. Kendrick and the rest of your team over at Strong did everything that I would've done."

"So there's nothing else you can do for me? No surgery or remedy or cream or something? I'm desperate."

Dr. Bennett offered a tight-lipped smile, still carrying herself with poise and grace while she delivered bad news. "I'm sorry, but realistically no surgery is going to return your skin to the way it was before your accident. Certainly no cream would. That might actually serve as a further irritant."

"So what am I supposed to do?" Ian asked loudly.

Her voice remained calm, her face showed no indication that he startled her in any way. "Have you tried seeing a counselor? Traumatic changes to one's appearance like this requires quite a level of adjustment. Something that will take time to accept."

"I will not accept this!" he shouted. "You're a *doctor*! You're supposed to be able to *help* people!"

"And I would if I could, but I'm afraid all options have been exhausted." She turned to the chart. "Let me have Paula at the front desk get you the contact information for a counselor I recommend. I think she'd be able to offer you some great coping—"

"I don't want to cope, I want to get my face back! Why can't you people understand that?"

"Mr. Coffed, I can certainly sympathize—"

"What about plastic surgery? At this point, I don't care if it's fake. I just need to get everyone to stop staring at me all the time. I want to look normal!"

"That is an option we could explore, but if I'm being honest, it's not one I have a lot of faith in," Dr. Bennet said. "Surgery such as that requires the skin to have a certain level of durability that yours has lost as a result of your injuries. The very composition of your skin has been altered—scarred. That makes treatments very difficult."

"I need something!" Ian grabbed the doctor by her coat and for the first time, fear showed on her face. "Look at me! Would you want to go around looking like *this*?"

"Mr. Coffed, please remain calm." She waited a beat, then said, "Let me go."

"Dr. Bennett, is everything okay in there?" a woman's voice asked from the other side of the door.

Ian pushed the doctor out of the way and swung the door open. The woman on the other side recoiled once she laid eyes on him. The reaction only made him snarl at her before he turned and stormed down the hall.

If it was the last thing he did, he was going to find a way to fix himself. And if none of these medical *professionals* wanted to help, he would have to look elsewhere.

CHAPTER 20

Samantha yanked on her door handle one more time to make sure it was locked. She looked both ways on the street and crossed to the sidewalk on the other side, pushing her wind-blown hair out of her face. The wind had a way of cutting right through her and giving her chills worse than the actual temperature. She kept her head down as she pressed on to the bakery. The quicker she got inside, the better.

"Samantha! Yoo-hoo!"

She looked up and saw Steven getting out of his car. He shut the door and came over to her on the sidewalk.

"You were in your own little world, weren't you?"

"I guess so." She she shook more hair out of her face before meeting his eyes. "Hey, before we go in there, I just want to say that I'm sorry for getting mad at you yesterday on the phone."

His brow furrowed, but he didn't say anything.

"Lately I've been short with your mother and I know she's only trying to help—in her own way," she went on. "I just felt like I wasn't being heard, but you were right. She is your mother and I'm going to have to learn how to navigate not being the only woman in your life. I'll figure it out. So, again, I'm sorry for being grumpy."

Steven flashed her a smile and waved his hand in her direction. "Don't worry about it. It's no big deal."

Samantha narrowed her eyes and was about to ask him what he meant by that, but behind them a car beeped from across the street. They turned and saw Mary step out of the car parked behind Samantha and rush over to greet them.

"All three of us here at the same time. What are the chances?"

Samantha offered a polite smile.

"Shall we go in?" Steven extended his arm out toward the entry of the bakery.

"Sure," Samantha said.

As they walked to the door, Mary reached for Samantha's arm. "Your sister couldn't make it, dear?"

Samantha shook her head. "No, she has a lot of homework she still needs to get to. She doesn't like to do it on the weekend."

"Oh, that's right. She's still in school."

"Y-Yeah, she is." Samantha didn't have time to elaborate

further and stand up for her sister.

"Interesting," Mary said pointedly. "You'd think she'd want to be here."

"Honestly, it's more of a bride and groom thing, so there's really no reason you should even be here either," Steven said.

Mary stopped and looked at him with wide eyes. Even Samantha was surprised to hear the words that were coming out of his mouth.

He smiled at them both and opened the door. "After you, ladies."

Mary lingered on her son a moment and then stepped in.

"Oh, it smells delicious in here!" Steven cooed.

The shop was small and long, with white tile and natural woodwork adorning the space. To the left of the door was a long display counter that featured various sweets and baked goods.

From behind the counter, a woman looked up and smiled. She had a black apron on that was coated in flour and her blonde hair was pulled back into a bun.

"Hi! Are you here for the cake testing?"

"That's us!" Steven announced. "What do you have for us?"

The woman behind the counter introduced herself as Leah and went through the options they had to choose from. Different flavors, different designs, and the many different layers. And each one came at various price levels, even though they all looked beautiful.

"Let me pull out some samples for you." Leah disappeared into the room at the end of the counter and came back a moment later with a tray. "Okay, so here we have the vanilla." She set out a small plate with tiny pieces of white cake. "And this is chocolate." Again, she put out another plate. "And these are our more funky flavors: lemon, spice, and almond." She placed a third plate beside the other two, all with different colored pieces of cake.

Steven and Samantha each reached for a piece. Mary hesitated, until Samantha waved her forward, giving her permission.

Maybe what Steven said to her outside actually worked, she thought. *A little rude, but if it did the trick…*

"What are your thoughts?" Samantha asked Steven as she took a bite of the final sample.

"The spice cake is my favorite, but I think if we wanted to go a little more funky—" He smirked up at Leah. "—but still stay pretty safe, we could go with the almond."

"The almond was actually one of my favorites," Samantha agreed. "And we're thinking probably fifty to seventy-five people, so how big of a cake would we need?"

"Oh, it's a smaller wedding," Leah said. "I like it. Um…I guess that would depend on how many layers you want."

"I think three would look nice," Steven said. "Maybe have some of that decorative frosting on it, too."

Samantha looked at the pictures Leah had pulled out for them. "Yeah, that would look good."

"Just remember to watch the cost," Mary said quietly from beside them. "The more details, the more work, and the higher the price tag."

Steven grumbled and turned to his mother. "Can you just back off? It's mine and Samantha's wedding. Not yours."

"Steven!" Samantha said as a warning.

"She's always butting into our decisions," he went on.

Mary looked stricken. "I just—I wasn't trying—"

Samantha grabbed his wrist and pulled him deeper into the bakery, back to the hallway by the bathrooms. It was the only way they could have even the illusion of privacy. "What's going on with you two?"

"What do you mean?"

"You've never talked to your mother like this before. It's not a side of you I'm liking right now."

"I'm sorry," he said with only a hint a sincerity. "I just love you and I want you to have the wedding you love."

"Well, I appreciate that, but you don't need to hurt your mother while—"

Her words were cut off when his lips pressed against her. His arms pulled her close to him, holding her there, pinning her. She pushed at his chest in an effort to free herself. They were never one of those couples who showed a lot of public affection, so where did this side of him come from?

When he finally pulled away, he smiled at her and then turned to return to the counter. Samantha stood back and looked at him with confusion.

CHAPTER 21

Ian held the door out for the witch and the older woman. He plastered on a smile, trying his best to emulate Steven, who he had been observing for a couple weeks now. The witch's fiancé seemed like he was a perfect—even to the point of nauseating—gentleman.

The old bag gave a curt wave before crossing the street. Ian tried to stifle a smile at the change in her demeanor, but he was too happy about it. The broad needed to be put in her place and he did exactly that. He only thought the witch would be more appreciative of it, but then, it seemed like she always had *something* to complain about. What a bitch. No wonder Steven was a whipped man.

"Are you coming back to the house?" Samantha asked.

Ian shook his head. "I have a few errands to run before I'll be over. Probably spend the night, though." There was another boyfriend to tend to so he could start to reel in the other witch.

"Kathy will be home." Samantha seemed to be searching his face for any hesitation.

"When isn't she?" Ian said with a short laugh.

"True. Her party-girl phase has dwindled a bit since she started school. Anyway, I ran to the bank before I came here, so I'm going to do some grocery shopping before I head home. I'm going to try to get it all done so I don't have to go anywhere tomorrow, but I'm sure I forgot to add something to the list."

Ian nodded. "See you later, then."

She leaned in for a kiss and once again, he couldn't help himself. Grabbing her, he pulled her in for a deeper kiss. This was one of his favorite parts of what he did—so many different lovers to choose from! All he needed to do was morph into different skin and everyone was so willing!

When they parted, the witch looked at him and for a brief moment, he was afraid he had somehow blown his cover. But she brushed it off, readjusted her purse on her shoulder, and told him she'd see him later.

Ian got back into Steven's car and waited for the witch to drive off before he started the engine. At the light, he turned left on State Street, then another left onto 3rd Street, heading in the opposite direction from Steven's house. He followed 3rd all the way down until it turned into Lookout Drive at Cascade Street.

Careful to park on the street, Ian grabbed what he needed and got out of the car to walk up to Milo's front door as if it was his daily routine. He even casually checked Milo's mailbox—and it was a good thing he did, too. At the bottom of the gold-plated metal box beside the front door, sat a house key.

He's just asking for someone to come in! Ian thought.

Without hesitation, Ian unlocked the front door and let himself in, careful to lock up behind him.

The house was smaller than it looked from the outside. Perhaps it was the furniture or the popcorn ceiling or the hideous floral wallpaper on the front wall of the house. Either way, Ian wasn't there to comment on the decor. He had work to do.

Kicking off Steven's shoes at the front door, Ian carried them as he made his way across the carpet. Best not to leave any trace behind.

Upstairs, the house was even smaller. There was a tiny back bedroom, smaller than some people's closets nowadays. It had a single twin bed that was made up with a blue plaid bedspread and an ornate dresser against the opposite wall that had a thick layer of dust on it. In the corner sat stacks of boxes marked "HIGH SCHOOL" and "PHOTOS" among other things.

At the front of the house was a room only slightly bigger than the other, but it was clear this is the one that was used. The double bed was unmade, a laundry basket sat in the corner with a few pieces of clothing laying on the floor beside it. The closet door was open, revealing the clothes in the perfectly organized order. Suits and business attire on one side, casual items in the middle, and paint-splattered, stained T-shirts and pants—still ironed and hung neatly—all the way on the other side.

Ian looked back at the hamper and laughed.

The clothes on the floor and the unmade bed are probably this fool's attempt to convince himself that he's not OCD, he thought. *Bet he's been thinking about this all day. The one part of his house that is out of order.*

Refocusing, Ian searched under the bed—nothing—and the bottom of the closet—nothing—for a bag or suitcase or something. Like with everyone, if he was going to wear Milo's skin, he needed to wear his clothes too.

Finally, in a small closet at the top of the stairs, Ian found a duffle bag folded neatly on a bottom shelf, among the linens that were stored in a similar fashion.

Ian was tempted to take the sheets and towels and throw them all over, just to make it feel less like a showroom and more like a house. But everything needed to be in perfect order until he could get to Milo, who would be home anytime now.

Taking the bag back to the bedroom, Ian opened the dresser drawer and pulled out armfuls of clothes and shoved them in the bag. At the moment, it didn't matter exactly what he grabbed, as long as it was Milo's. He went to the closet and began to do the same thing, but this took him longer. He needed to pull each of the items off the hangers.

He let out a groan of frustration and threw the hangers on the floor next to the closet. It wasn't much, but it made him feel better.

Outside, he heard the sound of a car door closing and he stepped to the window. Milo's car sat in the driveway and a few seconds later, Ian heard the front door open.

Smiling, he pulled out the rag he brought from the car and the bottle of chloroform. Dousing the rag, he ducked behind the bedroom door and waited for Milo to come up the stairs.

He knew he would. Milo had had the same routine day-after-day for the last week.

Sure enough, after the refrigerator door closed down in the kitchen, the faint creak of the stairs beneath the carpet sounded. Ian could sense Milo's presence. He wondered if that sense was reciprocated, but Milo stepped into his bedroom without any fear that there was anyone waiting for him.

And what a surprise that was for him.

Ian moved quick, coming up behind Milo. He restrained him with one hand and shoved the rag against his mouth and nose with the other. Milo struggled, but didn't put up as much of a fight as Steven did.

As the effects of the drug took hold, Milo sunk to the floor and Ian followed, holding the rag to his mouth just to be sure the impact would last.

With Milo passed out on the floor, Ian rushed downstairs to get the rope from Steven's car. The growing darkness would hide the item, but Ian would have to wait until it was fully dark to put Milo in the trunk. That would also require backing Steven's car into the driveway to make it easier.

Slipping on whatever shoes were by the door, Ian went out to the street, pulled the coil of rope out of the trunk, and returned to the house.

Back upstairs, he went to work tying up Milo's hands, then his ankles. Simply taking people hostage was a lot easier than murdering them. It all depended on how long he planned on using someone's skin, which would require keeping hostages alive longer. There was always the risk of escape, but in reality, who was going to believe there was a doppelgänger running around? A dead body is harder to ignore.

But sometimes murder was required. The trick was to make it seem like they hadn't been missing after all. That they just went on a long vacation and never returned.

With Milo's body secured, the next part was the hardest: moving him.

Ian tried his best to lift Milo over his shoulder, but his strength depended on the strength of the skin he was wearing. As it was, Steven apparently didn't have much. Not like some people whose skin he wore.

Instead, Ian resorted to dragging Milo. First, he grabbed his feet, but when Milo's head banged into the doorframe as he tried to make a turn, Ian decided that wouldn't work. Instead, he spun him around and hooked his hands in Milo's armpits and dragged him down the stairs, nearly toppling over backward on his way.

Dead weight was a bitch.

Stopping to catch his breath, Ian went into the kitchen and found the drawer with duct tape—everyone had duct tape. He slapped a piece over Milo's mouth, just in case. The sun looked like it would be setting soon, but the effects of the drug varied between people.

Going back for round two, Ian managed to drag Milo around to the back door, only stopping when he heard the doorbell ring.

Dropping Milo where he was, Ian peeked his head around the corner and tried to make out who it was through the sheer curtains on the windows. It was the other witch. Kathy.

And he still looked like Steven.

CHAPTER 22

Kathy paced back and forth on the front porch of Milo's house. She hadn't been able to focus on anything all day since he had dropped her off, which was really bad for getting her homework done. Without being able to talk to Samantha about it since she wasn't home yet, Kathy decided it was best to talk to Milo directly and she didn't want to do it over the phone.

It had been a few minutes since she rang the bell so she tried again and knocked on the door. Lifting up to her tiptoes, she looked through the window at the top of the door and saw some of the lights were on. And Milo's car was in the driveway.

Hopefully he hadn't seen her and decided to ignore her.

Kathy figured she should give him the benefit of the

doubt—something he hadn't exactly given her—and waited a bit longer. Out on the street, she looked out as several crunchy leaves blew in the wind, toward the cars parked on the opposite side. The one closest looked familiar, but her eyes were having a hard time placing it in the darkness.

Behind her, the door swung open and she jumped. She turned and saw Milo standing in the doorway. He was shirtless, only wearing a pair of sweatpants, and his chest was rising and falling quickly with short breaths.

"Are you okay?" she asked.

"Just doing a little, um, exercise," he said.

She didn't realize Milo exercised. As much as she tried to picture him sweating and huffing and puffing, she couldn't. He always seemed so…put together. Even though he had a fairly dirty job with the city.

"What do you want?"

Kathy bristled at the harshness of his question, but figured that was expected. "I want to talk to you about Harry."

"Harry?" Milo's eyes grew wide and his eyebrows shot up. After a second, they dropped and he asked in a more casual tone, "What about Harry?"

"I'll explain inside." She took a step forward, but he put his hand across the doorway, blocking her path. "What's the matter?"

"It's a bad time. I was going to…take a bath."

"You take baths?"

"Uh, yeah," he said. "Helps my muscles relax after working out."

Her eyes lingered over his bare chest, which bore only the slightest hint of muscle definition. Still, she nodded, convinced that he was lying. He just didn't want her to come inside and she couldn't blame him. Several hours ago when he dropped her off, if he had tried to follow her inside, she wouldn't have let him in either.

"Well, I really think we should talk," she said. "If there's going to be any kind of future with us, I think it's important."

He seemed to be reading her for something before he responded. "I know, but I still think I need more time."

"Okay. When do you think you'll be ready?"

Milo stepped back and reached for the door, clearly done with the conversation. "I don't know. Maybe tomorrow sometime. Goodnight, Kathy."

She opened her mouth to respond, but got the door shut in her face instead. That was *not* how she thought it would go. Anger fueled her and she reached her hand up to knock on the door again, but decided better of it and stepped away.

She could take a hint. Milo didn't want to talk to her. Message received. Now she needed to decide whether he was worth giving another shot or if she was done with him. This back and forth business wasn't working for either of them.

Stepping back onto the sidewalk, Kathy gave one last look at Milo's house before she continued walking into the darkness.

CHAPTER 23

- NOVEMBER 1983 -
CLEVELAND, OH

The room smelled of a mix of sandalwood and cigarettes. Ian sat in a chair with a broken support so that one cheek sunk lower than the other. There were only two other chairs like this in the small makeshift waiting room that had clearly once been this woman's front porch.

To say he was skeptical of this place, just as he had been of all the other holistic healers he'd visited in the last two months, would be a massive understatement. But he was desperate.

His knees bounced as he watched the clock, unsure if it was even working properly. The hoodie that had now become a part of his identity was pulled low to cover as much of his face as possible. Traveling to different cities meant he was subjected to new kinds of scrutiny—he didn't know which parts to avoid like he did back in Rochester. Even this holistic center was in a part of town that didn't give Ian the warm and fuzzies regardless of his appearance.

The door swung open suddenly and he jumped. A woman with short, curly blonde hair and makeup that was only slightly less than a clown stood in the doorway.

"Ian Coffed?" she called, as if there was anyone else waiting.

"That's me," he said, offering his hand.

"I'm Dalila Thatcher. Step into my office." Her voice was gravelly, lingering on a phlegmy cough. "I can see why you're here."

At least she's straight to the point, he thought. Not like the other holistic "healers" had been—too caught up in being polite to acknowledge the obvious. His face was messed up, among other deformities.

"I was hoping you'd be able to help me." Ian took a seat on a threadbare couch that very well could've been the source of the strange mix of scents filling the house. This room wasn't much better than the first—littered with magazines and drooping houseplants. Dark paisley curtains covered the windows, although there were several lamps lit so it wasn't dark.

Dalila took a seat behind her desk and reach for a box of cigarettes. "So tell me more about your journey with what you've got going on."

"Well, a little more than a year ago I woke up to my apartment on fire," he started. "Before I could get out, the ceiling collapsed and—"

"What did the fire department rule as the cause?" Her cigarette clung to her bottom lip as she took notes.

"I think they just said it was an accident."

"Sure, but what kind of accident? Electrical shortage? Blanket draped over a heater? Furnace backfiring?"

"I don't—I don't know."

She waved in his direction impatiently. "Go on. Talk to me about your doctors."

"Well I went to a burn specialist at Strong Memorial Hospital in Rochester. They assigned me a whole team of people. They tried skin grafts, nerve transplants, therapy, but nothing took. I still look like a freak."

Dalila raised her eyebrows and nodded. "Anyone else?"

"I went to a burn clinic at ECMC in Buffalo. Got the same news. They couldn't do anything more for me and they didn't want to entertain the idea of plastic surgery. Said my skin had been through enough and wouldn't sustain the trauma."

"Any other doctors?"

Ian shook his head.

Dalila made a note, then asked, "Am I the first holistic specialist you've seen?"

Definitely not. Along his way down to Cleveland, he had visited healers in Fredonia, NY, Warren, PA, and Youngstown, OH. After trying several of their so-called "remedies," which included salves and balms and ointments that only further irritated his fragile skin, Ian wrote them off as loonies. Each one of them recommended the next "healer," building skepticism in Ian while widening his eyes to the fact that more people believed in spirits and auras than he ever thought possible.

"Hardly," Ian said with a laugh. He recounted his dealings with the other non-professional specialists, ending his tale with an honest impression of the whole thing. "I think you're all full of crap, if I can be frank. I don't think you have any idea what really is going to work on me and I'm getting tired of being a guinea pig."

"Then why are you here?"

He sighed, studying the faded pattern on the arm of the couch as a way to stall for time. "I'm desperate."

"I see." She turned her attention to her notes, then turned around and pulled a book off the bookshelf behind her. She propped her cigarette between two fingers as she flipped through the pages.

"So what do you think? Are you going to make me a lab rat too or are you going to be honest with me and say you can't help me?"

Dalila ignored him at first, reading through a passage in the book. Finally, she said, "Neither. In fact, I think I'm the one person who *can* help you, but it requires you to have an open mind."

"I'm sitting in a hippie's living room and she's *not* the first one I've seen," Ian replied. "I think my mind's already pretty open."

"All right then. What I'm about to tell you, you need to listen carefully and hear me out. Are you sure you can do that?"

He scoffed and rolled his eyes. He would've crossed his arms if he could still bend that way. "Yes, I think I can manage."

"Those other healers weren't fully truthful with you. They were witches, as am I."

"Witches? Are you kidding me?" He struggled to rise to his feet.

Dalila waved her cigarette at him as she motioned for him to sit back down. Smoke dissipated through the air. "You told me you could have an open mind about this."

Ian opened his mouth to retort, but thought better of it and stayed quiet.

"Yes, we're witches," she went on, "and from what I know, and based on what you told me about your doctors' failed attempts to fix you, I would have to say that that attack on your home last year was not a mistake."

Ian sat forward, suddenly interested. "You think it was arson? Why?"

"I can't answer that," Dalila replied. "However, if traditional medical remedies were unable to address your difficulties, I think we may be looking at a supernatural attack."

Once again, he rolled his eyes and sat back in his seat. "Okay, I'll play along. If this was supernatural, what kind of *magical* remedy do you have that can fix me? Because, I gotta be honest, I'm not looking forward to putting anything else on my skin. The last few attempts have left permanent scars."

"What I'm thinking should be ingested. A potion. I'll need a day to craft it, but it should fight off the effects of the magical flame that gave you those scars."

"You want me to drink something you cooked up in your kitchen?"

"So far you've applied unidentified ointment to yourself without question. Why is my alternative such a concern?"

"Because I don't want to get burned again!" he shouted. Then, quietly, "No pun intended."

"You have my word that this potion will not harm you," she said. "It is not my intention to cause pain. I'm a healer, it'd be bad for business if you ended up worse off after having seen me."

"How much is this going to cost me?"

"Depends on the materials I need. Come back tomorrow at the same time. I'll have the potion ready for you then."

As Ian walked out of Dalila's ramshackle office, he didn't have a doubt in his mind that she was loony just as the rest of the holistic healers had been. But among that skepticism was a grain of hope that maybe her crazy potion would actually work and he could be himself again.

Maybe, in twenty-four hours' time, he'd be on the road to normal again.

CHAPTER 24

The door at the top of the stairs opened and both Steven and Harry strained against their restraints to see who it was. They waited in anticipation as the view on the stairs changed. First, just a shadow, then a sneaker-clad foot as it descended the stairs backwards, and finally the loud bang as yet another person was dragged down to the cement floor, bound in ropes at his hands and feet.

Even through the darkness—and the distressed look on the prisoner's face—Steven recognized Milo. He had only met Kathy's boyfriend a handful of times in passing, but it made sense that the "psycho," as Harry put it, would go after both of the guys currently dating the sisters.

Yet that still didn't explain why Harry was here.

What was even stranger was that Milo was being dragged down the stairs by…Milo. Like when Harry said Steven was dragged down here by someone who looked just like his twin.

"Milo!" Steven called out once he saw he was awake.

The new prisoner struggled a little in the restraints, but mostly he just gritted his teeth as his body took each of the hits down the stairs. He lay limply on the cement floor once they reached the bottom.

The other Milo—the cleaner-looking one—went to his prisoner's feet and cut through the binds. Ignoring Steven and Harry, he moved to a space in the rafter several feet down from Steven and worked a strand of rope through. Tying one end to the restraints on Milo's hands, the second Milo began to hoist him up using the rafter as a pulley system.

"Milo, fight back!" Steven called out. "Kick him! Get to your feet and run!" He expected retaliation from the second Milo, but none came.

Milo groaned as the ropes around his wrists dragged him across the floor and lifted him. He struggled to get to his feet, finally finding his balance. He swung one leg back toward the second Milo and actually made contact, but other than giving some extra slack to the rope, the other Milo held his ground.

"That's enough out of you," he said in a voice that somehow sounded more sinister than what Steven remembered from Milo's regular voice. Perhaps that was only the circumstances darkening his tone, though.

The second Milo hoisted up the original one until he stood with his arms raised, just like the other two captives.

"Are you okay?" Harry called out quietly.

Milo grunted in response.

The second Milo clapped the dirt off his hands and cast a quick glance in Steven and Harry's direction, checking to make sure they were still tied up. Satisfied, he turned to ascend the stairs.

"You can't just leave us here!" Steven called out. His heart was pounding and the fearful voice in his head kept screaming, *Shut up! Let him go! You'll be safer if he's gone!* But Steven thought of Samantha and what she would do in a situation like this and he knew she wouldn't just sit quietly as she was taken prisoner. He wasn't about to do the same.

"Whoever you are, let us go," he went on.

The second Milo turned and quickly crossed the room until he was inches away from Steven, who couldn't even take a step back.

"Don't worry," the second Milo said with a sneer. "I'm not going to kill *you*. I just need to borrow your identities for a little while."

"Then why tie us up? Why not just lock us in a room somewhere?" If they didn't have the restraints, they'd have a better chance of breaking free. They'd certainly have more strength in their arms.

The second Milo took a step back and made a face. "I've

tried that before. Didn't work. You give them too much time to think and they'll come up with something to make your life miserable. And tying you up is easier than killing you, although I'm not opposed to that."

He stepped over to the tall freezer in the corner and opened it. Inside, crammed in like a pretzel, was Ruby Harding, Samantha and Kathy's neighbor. Her skin was white, ice coating the delicate features of her face. Worst of all, though, was the blood coating her nightgown.

"A few days observing her and her husband and I knew they'd both be a problem," the other Milo explained. He shut the door and stepped back to the stairs. "I imagined she'd be a screamer. Someone you couldn't quite silence, even with threats. And her husband needed to die because if he saw her screaming, he would've done the same. Humans are pack-like creatures, you know that? We do what we see other people doing. Even if it's stupid."

"What are you trying to accomplish?" Steven asked, even though he was afraid he already knew the answer.

The imposter fired a finger gun at Steven with a *click* sound coming from the corner of his mouth. "You'll see! It takes work to maintain my bag of tricks." Steven gritted his teeth, not sure what else to say. Clearly, Harry had dubbed this guy with the correct moniker: psycho. And he wasn't going to let them go anytime soon, if at all.

"Now, if you'll excuse me, I have to keep your lady-friend

company." The second Milo started climbing the stairs. "I'll be back to feed you later!"

When he reached the top of the stairs, the door closed with a sound that rang out into the basement, telling the men that they were trapped. And in serious trouble.

CHAPTER 25

Are you *sure* you saw him in class on Wednesday?" Samantha pulled cans of soup out of the brown paper bag and stacked them in the pantry cabinet. She left two out on the counter for dinner.

"Yes!" Kathy exclaimed. She was adding cups of yogurt to the drawer in the fridge. She had just gone over the story with Samantha, how Harry's parents said he'd been missing since Tuesday. "I talked to Harry on Wednesday. I remember, because he asked me out and I blew him off, remember?"

Samantha shot her sister a look. "Of course that's how you'd remember."

"Well, it wasn't a run-of-the-mill day." Kathy closed the drawer, then the fridge door, and started folding up the paper bag. "So anyway, now I think Milo's mad at me because I brought him to some other boy's house."

Samantha grabbed the last bag of groceries and pulled out the produce she got: bananas, lettuce, tomatoes, apples. "Can you blame him? It was kind of rude."

"It's not like I called him up and asked him to take me directly to Harry's," Kathy countered. "He showed up at school when I was already on my way over to his house. What was I supposed to do?"

Samantha shrugged and folded up the last bag, passing it off to her sister, who stuffed it with the rest of the paper bags in the cabinet below the counter. "Why did you say you *think* Milo's mad at you?"

"Well, we had an argument after we left Harry's house," Kathy explained. "He insinuated that maybe I was hiding Harry somewhere—"

"Are you kidding me?"

"Nope. So that's why when he tried to apologize when he dropped me off, I shut the door in his face—well, sort of."

"Good." Samantha opened a can of soup with a can opener, wincing as she struggled to cut through the metal. "If he's going to talk to you like that, then I'd say just be done with him."

Kathy sighed. "I know. But I was thinking about it all day and I thought I didn't give him a chance to fully explain himself."

"Accusing you of keeping a boy hidden is a big accusation.

What does he think? You *kidnapped* him?"

"I don't think he meant it like *that*," Kathy said. "Only psychos tie up people and hold them hostage. I think he just meant that maybe I knew where Harry was and I wasn't telling anyone because I wanted to keep his secret."

With the lid off, Samantha dumped the contents of the soup can in a pot and shot her sister another look. "Still not great, Kath."

"It was the heat of the moment. He was mad. I think I can cut him some slack. Which is why I went over to his house earlier to apologize."

"How'd that go?" Samantha got started on the second can.

"Not great, not terrible. He seemed…odd. Maybe it was just bad timing, I don't know. But it felt like he couldn't wait to get me off his porch."

"Maybe he's still mad."

"That's what I figured, which would explain the weird behavior."

"I think it's a full moon thing or something. Steven's been acting weird lately too."

"How so?"

Samantha filled the empty can of soup with water and poured it into the pot. "It's hard to explain. It's just a feeling I have."

"Well, as much as things with me and Milo are weird right now, my biggest concern is where Harry is."

"I know he's your friend, Kathy, but unless he was taken magically, it's not your job to find him," Samantha said. "When you talked to his parents, did you get the feeling that magic was involved?"

Kathy leaned forward on her hands. "No."

"Then I think you should just leave it alone and let the police handle it. They did call them, right?"

"Of course they did. But it's been more than forty-eight hours and the likelihood that he'll be returned home safely are very slim now. I just keep picturing the look on his mother's face! She was so upset."

"I can't even imagine," Samantha said. "But unfortunately, people are abducted all the time without any connection to magic. This is just one of those instances where it hits closer to home. Are they organizing a search party or anything?"

"I don't know. It didn't sound like it. It might be too late. Or they just don't know where to even start looking. Until I said I saw him on Wednesday, they had no idea when he was last seen."

"Have you talked to the police to give a statement?"

"Yeah, they called this afternoon. They just wanted to verify that I saw him, ask which school, what class, that kind of thing. They're going to check with Roger and do some digging there if any leads come up."

"Hopefully they find something," Samantha offered. "If nothing else, his parents at least need closure."

The front door opened and Steven called out, "Hello? Is anyone home?"

"In the kitchen!" Samantha shouted back.

A few moments later, he stepped in looking very unkempt for his usual appearance. The dress shirt he wore to the office was untucked and his skin glistened with perspiration, which caused his shirt to cling to his chest.

"Did you go for a run or something?" Samantha asked. "Why didn't you change?"

"What?" Steven looked down. "Oh, no. My, uh, thermostat was on the fritz. Just needed new batteries, but it was blowing out hot air all day long, so my apartment was like the gates of hell."

Kathy snickered.

Samantha hooked an eyebrow. "And you didn't change your clothes there if you were sweating?"

"I have clothes here too," he said. "Besides, I wanted to take a shower. Why do you look so confused?"

She shook her head. "I guess I am. I thought you were running errands?"

"I had to go pick up batteries," he said. "For the thermostat. Geez, you act like you don't trust me."

"No, it's not—" Samantha's words were cut off when he came around the island and wrapped his sweaty body against hers, planting his wet kiss on her lips. Knowing that her efforts to push him away would be futile, she remained still until he pulled back. "Steven, would you stop doing that?"

"Loving you?"

Kathy snorted.

Samantha shot her a look.

"I'm going to go up and take a shower," he said. "I'll be down shortly."

When he left the room and Samantha was sure he had disappeared upstairs, she turned back to her sister and said, "See? He's acting weird!"

"I think it's sweet," Kathy said. "You guys still have that spark. I think with all this wedding planning, he's just getting excited about becoming your husband."

"Yeah, but it's not the way he usually acts."

Kathy shrugged. "People change."

"But kisses don't. And his have been…different."

"Well, before you jump to conclusions over a *kiss*, I'd say you should talk to him first. Just tell him you're not into being mauled like that. He'll understand."

"That's the thing, though." Samantha looked toward the door where Steven had departed. "As my fiancé, he should already know."

CHAPTER 26

*W*hat a picturesque morning, Ian thought to himself. He fixed the creases in the newspaper to fold it to the next page. *The sun is streaming through the window, the smell of coffee is wafting in the air, and I'm sitting across from a beautiful woman who I shared a bed with last night.*

He looked up at Samantha and smiled. She was wearing pajama pants and a thin black sweater. When she looked at him, her eyes lacked any burst of emotion they talk about in the movies when you look at someone you love. Ian told himself it was because she was still tired.

A small part of him worried that she was beginning to see through the façade of his Steven impersonation. But then, if that were the case, why would she be having coffee with him?

Either way, he needed to kill her.

"Morning!" Kathy trilled as she came into the kitchen. She went over to the fridge and pulled out a cup of yogurt. "I couldn't sleep that well last night. Kept thinking about Harry, which then turned into thinking about Milo." She reached into a drawer and pulled out a spoon. "Ugh, why do men have to be so difficult?" Her eyes flicked up to Ian. "No offense."

He put up his hands. "None taken."

"Please don't tell me you're going to do something stupid." Samantha downed the last bit of her coffee and carried the mug and the plate to the sink.

Kathy shoveled yogurt into her mouth and murmured around the spoon, "I just want to talk to him."

"Milo? Are you sure you want to do that?"

"Yeah. He was acting strange yesterday only because emotions were so fresh, you know? But the adult thing to do is to talk to him about it. We won't get past this if we don't talk."

"And what if he doesn't want to talk?" Samantha asked. "He didn't last night."

Kathy sighed before scooping the last bit of yogurt in her mouth. "Then I guess that's my answer."

Samantha sighed.

"What?"

"I just don't think it's a good idea if he thinks you're a kidnapper."

"A what?" Ian asked.

The girls ignored him.

"That's why we need to talk," Kathy said. "I hope he wants to apologize for what he said."

"I don't think you're going to get the answer you want," Samantha muttered.

"A girl can hope, right?"

"Good luck." Samantha ran the hot water and reached for the sponge. "Do you want to take my car?"

Ian sat at the table watching the events unfold as his heart raced. He needed to get to Milo's house before the witch. And he needed to have enough time to morph back into him and make it look like he'd just woken up. He fanned the opening of his robe, feeling a flush of warmth overwhelm him.

Kathy tossed her spoon in the sink and reached for a banana on the counter. "That'd be gr—"

"Wait a minute," Samantha said quickly. "I totally forgot. I have a couple more places to run this morning."

"Darn."

"I could drop you off," she offered. "You'll have to wait for me to get ready. Maybe like half an hour."

"No, that's okay. I don't know how long I'll be with him and I don't want to have to wait for you to pick me up. I guess the bus it is then."

"Sorry." Samantha set a clean dish on a towel beside the sink.

"It's okay. Thanks anyway. Hope this goes well!"

The younger sister left the kitchen just as quickly as she came in.

Ian rose to his feet and stepped to the other side of the island. "Babe, I just remembered, I need to run home for some things."

"Again? You were just there last night. You didn't get what you needed then?"

"No, my, uh, upstairs neighbor called early this morning and said it sounded like there might be a water leak in my apartment."

Over her shoulder, Samantha stared at him with narrowed eyes. "Your upstairs neighbor? The one you complain about all the time because they have lead feet?"

Ian shrugged. "We're still neighbors."

"And this water leak just happened to come after your thermostat broke yesterday?"

She's putting it together. I may need to kill her sooner than later. Which means I'll need to kill the other witch soon too. I might not have time to free the hostages in the basement before I take off.

If he had to kill the three hostages he had, plus the two witches, plus the two bodies he already had stuffed in the freezer, that would be seven people killed in one quiet neighborhood. Surely that would make the news. Even with the ability to change his skin, it was a prospect that Ian didn't like.

Turning back to the sink, Samantha shook her head and

muttered, "You need to get out of that apartment. It's falling apart."

Ian breathed out the tension that was building up inside him. He forced a chuckle. "Yeah. So I'm going to take off. No telling what kind of damage water is doing."

"If you need to borrow our shop vac, it's in the basement."

"Thanks," he said, anxious to get out the door. "I'll check it out and let you know if I need it."

"Are you coming back here after?"

"I don't know." He stood in the doorway of the kitchen and looked longingly toward the rest of the house. He didn't know how quickly Kathy would get to Milo's, or how much time he'd need. "Maybe not. I might just meet you at the party later."

"That late?"

"Water leaks are nothing to scoff at." He came up behind her and kissed her cheek, deciding to lay off the affection a little. He didn't want to give her any other reason to suspect he might not actually be her lover. "Okay, I have to go. I'll see you later!"

Still in his robe, he raced to the front of the house. At the door, he slipped Steven's sneakers on his bare feet, grabbed his keys and swung open the door. From the kitchen, he heard Samantha call out, "Love you!"

CHAPTER 27

Even on a Saturday, the bus was not Kathy's favorite place to be. By time she got off at Gridley Park, the morning sun had been obscured by hazy clouds that was typical for October in Erie. As she turned onto Lookout Drive, a light drizzle had even begun to fall. She was grateful when she got under the cover of Milo's porch.

Hoping for a better outcome than she had the previous night, she rang the doorbell and waited for Milo to answer. When he did, he was wrapped in a white bathrobe and wore black socks.

Kathy smiled. "Oh wow. The only other guy that I know of who wears a bathrobe is my sister's boyfriend. He has one just like that."

Milo patted the soft cotton. "Oh, sorry. I was about to hop in the shower."

"Can we talk?" she asked.

He held the door open for her wider and stood aside to allow her to step through. "Come in."

As soon as she crossed the threshold, she felt the warmer, dryer air of the house surround her. The room was still dark, as if Milo hadn't been downstairs yet that morning.

He closed the door behind her and walked over to the kitchen. "Do you want coffee?"

She thought of her meager breakfast and nodded. "That'd be great. Thanks."

"No problem." Milo flicked a switch on the wall in the kitchen and nothing happened. He tried two more before the lights above shone bright.

Kathy took a seat at the small dining table and folded her hands. "I wanted to apologize for yesterday with what happened at Harry's house."

"Harry?" Milo spun around and stared at her with wide eyes. "Have you talked to him?"

She furrowed her brow. "No. I'm talking about what happened when we went to his house. How his parents were upset. You were there."

He stared at her with wide eyes a moment longer, then shook his head and smiled. "Right. Sorry. I'm out of it this morning. Still tired." He opened a drawer, then closed it.

Opened another one, closing it again.

"I can tell," she said with a laugh. "Did you forget where everything is in your kitchen? You're not moving like the expert you were two days ago."

Milo offered her a sheepish smile. He opened a cabinet and finally found the coffee grounds that he'd been looking for. He added them to the coffee maker and hit start before coming over to join Kathy at the table.

"Anyway," she continued. "I think yesterday was just a big misunderstanding. I say we just erase it from our memories. We were both wrong and there's no correcting that."

He nodded.

"But you did bring up some valid points," she said. "I haven't been fully committing to this relationship. So from now on, I'm going to try to be more of a girlfriend to you."

Before she could talk herself out of it, she grabbed the front of Milo's robe and pulled him in for a kiss. A real kiss. The kind that most couples wouldn't still get nervous about two months into a relationship.

Except, the kiss was different. Not the way she remembered it from when they kissed at the club. Truthfully, that was the last time they had properly kissed.

This kiss didn't give her the butterflies in her stomach. Didn't bring a smile to her face. It fell flat. And Kathy wondered if she had made a mistake telling him that she'd be his girlfriend before she gave him the kiss test.

Maybe Samantha had a point. Kissing said a lot about a guy and whether there was a future with him.

When they parted, Kathy felt as if she had already committed to her words, so decided to finish what else she came to say. "My neighbor is having a party tonight. I guess it's a combination Halloween and housewarming party. You should come."

Milo's face was hard to read. He still had a confused look from the kiss, but a hint of a smile was evident at the corners of his lips.

"I mean, I know it's last minute," Kathy went on, "so if you can't make it, I totally understand. I just thought it might be fun for the two of us—"

"Yes, absolutely!" he said. "That sounds like a lot of fun! I have plans during the day today, but I can meet you there."

She smiled. "Great! It's the house right across the street from us. You don't need to wear a costume or anything—unless, of course, you want to."

"I want to look my best for you." He leaned toward her, his robe parting a little as he did.

Kathy couldn't help but try to sneak a peek at his toned chest. Maybe he exercised after all.

Suddenly, he was kissing her again with just as much vigor as the first time. It felt nice, but still no butterflies. She liked Milo, but all signs kept telling her that she only liked him because she was trying to. Nothing about their relationship felt natural.

She pulled away. "I think the coffee might be done."

Kathy spent the next half hour chit-chatting with Milo. They talked about the party, about work, Kathy's classes. Surface talk. Still. Despite Kathy's declaration that she was going to start acting more like his girlfriend, they remained in a getting-to-know-each-other phase. After two months, she thought they'd be past big stuff. Their whole relationship had been talking and nothing else.

Not that she was ready for anything else.

With the coffee gone and their well of small talk depleted, Kathy suggested that she get out of Milo's hair and let him get going with his plans for the day. At the door, he kissed her again—trying very hard to impress her—but once again, she didn't feel anything special.

As she descended the stairs of his front porch, she was happy that the rain had at least stopped, although the sky was still overcast. She looked up and noted how few leaves were left on the trees. If it kept raining, they would fall sooner than later. She liked to see all of the colors.

On the street, her eyes landed on one car in particular. She thought it might've been the same one she saw the last time she came to Milo's. It looked familiar, almost as if she knew it. Yet she still couldn't put her finger on it. Weirder yet, she was compelled to investigate further.

Looking up and down the street for anyone who might be

outside, she crossed to the other side and walked up to the car. It was a small little Ford Escort. Silver. The license plate didn't ring any bells, but Kathy never really paid attention to any of that. Samantha probably would. Her brain was more attuned to numbers.

At the thought of Samantha, she remembered why the car looked so familiar: Steven had one just like it. She peeked inside, wondering if it was the same one. Nothing she saw through the windows indicated if it was Steven's. Then again, she deduced that she didn't know much about Steven's car to determine if it even was his.

And why would it be? As far as she knew, he was probably back at the house. She could ask him when she got home if she remembered.

Taking another look up and down the street, Kathy figured she should stop being a creeper and move along. She pushed away the feeling that it meant something. Her perceptions had been way off lately.

Besides, she knew that if she owned a car, she wouldn't take lightly to someone peeking in the windows.

CHAPTER 28

How pathetic do we look, showing up without our dates?" Samantha asked her sister as they exited their house. The older sister was dressed in a black dress and matching heels. Her brown hair hung on her shoulders, although she continuously reached up to it to swat it away from her face.

Kathy shut the door behind her and slid the key into the lock. She wore a much shorter—and tighter—red dress and her hair was pulled back in a bun on top of her head. Her eyes were heavily done up in makeup and she wore dark lipstick, which helped give her the vixen look she was going for. "Well, it's still early. So we'd look pathetic even if we had dates."

Samantha shot her sister a look and shivered in the breeze. She had wanted to wear a coat, but Kathy had told her that would ruin her look. She didn't argue further because the party *was* just across the street.

"It's weird that both Steven and Milo gave us the same answer." Kathy hooked her arm in her sister's and walked over to the Harding's.

"Add that to the list of weird things they've done lately," Samantha murmured. Kathy had told her how Milo had been different today when she went to see him. But the thing that Samantha couldn't get out of her mind was the feeling that Steven was lying to her. She didn't want to enter into a marriage if he was going to be unfaithful. Or sneaky. And she didn't want to accuse him without proof, but actions spoke louder than words sometimes.

"It's not that weird," Kathy said. "We can't force them to live together in one big house. We tried that before, remember?"

Samantha raised her eyebrows and thought back to when she and her sister faced the Siren. Their forced cohabitation cost Kathy her relationship with Jeremy and nearly cost Samantha hers with Steven.

"They have their own separate lives," Kathy went on. "Besides, you're the lucky one. Steven's had a track record of changing his plans to fit the ones you've come up with."

"You act like I control his life!"

They approached the steps leading to the front door of the Harding house. The railing was adorned with purple lights and several pumpkins sat on the sides of the front steps opposite two bouquets of red mums.

"I just thought they'd meet us at our house first," Samantha continued.

"We're literally across the street," Kathy said. "I don't think they'll get lost."

"I'm just saying, Steven's not acting like his normal self and I don't like it." Samantha knocked on the door. Only a few seconds later, it swung open and Eli Harding stood on the other side.

"Hey there! So good that you guys could make it!" He leaned in for a hug, which both sisters were startled by. The result was an awkward, distant, over the shoulder reach-around. When Eli pulled away, he stood back and took in their outfits. "Wow! You both look incredible!"

Samantha suddenly felt self-conscious and nervously shifted her weight.

Meanwhile, Kathy peered over Eli's shoulder and said, "Looks like you have a good turnout."

There was a decent crowd inside and a few of them were dancing along to the music blaring from the stereo set. Only a handful of them wore costumes. Pirates and zombies and princesses all mingling together. Samantha didn't recognize any of them, but then, she figured Eli And Ruby probably invited everyone they knew so she wouldn't know them all.

Eli looked inside and said, "Yeah, a lot of folks have shown up, which is nice." He stood aside and waved them forward.

"Well, come on in! Join the fun! We have candy and popcorn and punch. Even some apples in a bucket if you wanted to go bobbing."

Samantha gave him a polite smile. They didn't spend all that time getting ready just to bend over and shove their face in water. That seemed like a good way to have a horrible time.

"We also have the adult usuals," he went on. "Beer in the cooler, some liquor over at the wet bar with some mixers."

"Sounds good," Kathy said. "Is Ruby around? Thought she might be greeting people at the door."

"Yeah, she's somewhere around here." He scanned the room over the heads of the crowd.

Samantha saw her way out of the conversation and quickly said, "I'll go find her." She disappeared deeper into the house before Eli—or Kathy—could say anything otherwise.

CHAPTER 29

- JANUARY 1984 -
CLEVELAND, OH

I t's been about two months since you've started taking the remedy." Dalila sat behind her desk and took a puff of her cigarette, as if she were having a casual conversation with an old friend and not a client. "How do you feel?"

Ian clenched his jaw. "I feel the same."

"Hmm. You've been taking it as I've prescribed?"

"Yes! It smells like piss—and quite frankly probably tastes just like it too—but I still gag it down each morning."

"And there's been no change to your skin?"

"I didn't say that." He gently pulled back the sleeve of his sweatshirt to reveal his shiny, splotchy arm. There were angry red spots up and down. Some of them had the slightest tingle of an itch. Ian figured it'd be worse if his nerves weren't dead. "My skin is getting worse! I don't want to take it anymore. I'm done."

Dalila sat forward and studied his outstretched arm. "It's always like this? It never changes?"

Ian waved her cigarette smoke out of his face and sat back as he fixed his sleeve. "What do you mean?"

"Your skin. Does it always look like that?"

"Uh, I don't know if you heard, but I was in an accident—"

She waved her hand. "It was no accident. But we're talking about your skin right now. Answer the question."

"Of course it's—" He stopped. The obvious answer wasn't so obvious. His skin was different since he started seeing Dalila, but he couldn't quite describe the phenomenon. It only happened at rare moments. Actually, with as annoyed as he was feeling now with Dalila, he wouldn't be surprised if it started now.

"I can see in your eyes that something *has* changed!" she croaked with a yellow grin. "Yes, tell me. What is this change?"

"Sometimes my skin…looks rubbery and then it…I don't know, it sort of…bubbles."

"Bubbles?"

"Yes, and water doesn't seem to do anything for it!" It usually happened when he looked in the mirror and hated what he saw. Since he'd been staying in a hotel for the last two months, using up what was left of his savings account, he hadn't been able to remove the mirrors like he did in his apartment back in Rochester. And the cheap hotel he was staying at used plenty of mirrors to make the room look bigger, which meant that Ian saw himself often.

And hated himself often.

The thought of it brought that familiar feeling to the pit of his stomach—or rather, to his belly.

Dalila noticed his face and asked, "What is it? Is it happening now?"

Slowly, Ian stood and reach for the hem of his sweatshirt and pulled it up. Three small bubbles had begun to pop up on his belly.

Dalila laughed and cackled, jumping to her feet and clapping her hands. "Ah ha! That's it! That's how you know the potion has taken effect!"

Her laughter only made Ian angrier. He dropped his shirt down and shouted, "What are you talking about?"

The witch ignored him and continued to laugh.

Ian could feel the bubbles multiply underneath his clothes, but he didn't draw attention to it. They were spreading faster than they ever had before. Then again, he'd never been this angry or upset with his appearance. Dalila's laughter brought back bad memories of all the people who had laughed at him for the way he looked since the fire.

"Would you knock it off! What the hell did you do to me?"

Dalila dropped her cigarette in the ash tray and came around the desk. She placed her hands on his cheeks and stared into his eyes. "I've given you a gift!"

"A *gift*? Have you completely lost your marbles, lady?"

She rocked her head to the side, as if it were a possibility, but went on, "You now have the ability to look like someone else!"

"What are you talking about? I came to you because I wanted to look like *me*! The way I was before!"

She took a step back and waved toward herself. "Come on. Use this emotion to try to emulate my appearance."

Ian scowled as best he could with his taut skin. "I don't want to look like you."

"It's an experiment! If you don't believe I've been successful, what harm could it do to humor an old woman?"

Pushing his skepticism aside, Ian closed his eyes and tried to take on Dalila's appearance. He had no idea what he was doing, but he focused on her image in his mind—not a pretty thing to focus on—and soon after he felt the bubbles from his stomach grow all over his body, spreading like a new skin.

"Ah ha!" Dalila cheered. "That's it! You're doing it! It's like looking in a mirror!"

Ian opened his eyes and looked down. His belly suddenly bulged, pressed tight against his sweatshirt, his hair had grown long and straggly, as had his nails. The biggest and most exciting change, however, was that he *felt* all of these changes. Felt the soft cotton of his sweatshirt on his skin, Dalila's coarse hair on his face, his fingers as they pressed into his palms.

Well, not *his* fingers, but he was still elated that he could feel again.

"This is…" Ian tugged at the long hair resting on his chest.

Dalila waved him toward a mirror. "Come look! Come look! You have my appearance now, just as I said the potion would help you do!"

Ian stared in the mirror and for once he recoiled for a different reason. Instead of the scarred, broken man staring back at him, he saw a spitting image of Dalila. His eyes looked back and forth between the mirror and her, but there was no doubting it. This wasn't a sleight of hand or an illusion, this was what he looked like.

"How…? So I can change into *anyone*?"

She nodded. "I believe so, yes."

"For how long?"

Tossing up her hands, she cackled again. "Who knows! This is my first time trying this potion! But if you've been experiencing these bubbles for a while and still been taking the potion, I would think the effects of the magic are now permanent. You're welcome!" She left his side and danced around the room.

Ian stared back in the mirror. Was this the solution he was looking for? To appear like other people and not himself? Was that something he was willing to trade to no longer look like a freak?

Dalila didn't help him. She changed him. She pursued her own agenda at his expense. As if he wasn't human and worthy of the attention he was asking for. Didn't he have a right to live a somewhat normal life? She had only changed him from one freak into another.

To make matters worse, Dalila continued to cheer around him. As if she were his savior. As if she had listened to exactly what he had asked her to do.

She needed to know that her efforts—and all the efforts of all the witches he saw before her—only served to impair him further. Not to mention the witch who supposedly started the fire.

Turning, he reached for Dalila's throat and slammed her against the wall. For the first time, fear showed in her eyes.

"So this is what I am now?"

Wordlessly, she nodded.

"How certain are you that the fire was started by a witch?"

She choked and he lightened his grip, but only slightly. "I can't say for sure, but if the cause of the fire was left undetermined—and after seeing what it did to your skin—I think it's safe to say it was started by a witch. But I don't know who would—"

The rest of her words were cut off as Ian used his free hand to drive a knife into her stomach. He had picked it up from one of the tables near the mirror. It looked ceremonial, but it still had a point. Still got the job done.

As Dalila's body slumped to the floor, Ian stood over it in her appearance. He knew he had just crossed a line. Just turned into a murderer. But the act empowered him for the first time in nearly a year and a half.

Besides, what difference did it make if he murdered someone? It's not like anyone would apprehend him. He would just have to change his appearance and the police would be none the wiser. And didn't he deserve to make the so-called *witches* suffer for what they'd done to him? From the fire to the painful remedies to the potion that further solidified him as a freak.

All the witches responsible for his new life needed to die.

CHAPTER 30

"We're never getting out of here, are we?" Milo leaned forward weakly, relying on the restraints around his wrists to keep him up.

The ambient noise above them had grown loud as the Halloween party began. They heard footsteps and laughter and the steady beat of music. All of it created distractions from their screams.

"Don't talk like that." Steven wiggled his wrists as best he could to try to loosen the rope. His skin was burning, his arms were sore, and sweat dripped down his face. But he was determined. "We need some optimism. He said he wasn't going to kill us."

"Then how do you explain the people in the freezers?" Harry chimed in.

Steven's eyes darted over to the other side of the basement. He didn't have an explanation for that, other than the fact that the psycho could be lying. He probably *was* lying. Even more reason for them to get out sooner than later.

Before Steven could come up with his own lie to pacify the group, the door at the top of the stairs burst open, then shut quickly. Hurried feet pitter-pattered quickly as they descended the stairs.

"Good evening, gentlemen," the psycho said in Eli Harding's skin. "Enjoying yourself?" He stepped over to the corner, where there were several duffel bags lined near the staircase. He had brought them down earlier when he mercifully gave them dinner. If you could count rice cakes and crackers followed by a full bottle of water all at once as dinner.

"Let us go," Steven said. "You have a house full of people. We could call out for help."

The man who looked like Eli pulled off his green sweater and tossed it on top of one of the bags. "I told you, if you make a peep, you'll end up in the freezer like the other two." He pulled off his undershirt. "We're having a party! The neighbors won't suspect a thing if there's a few extra trash bags at the curb in the morning."

Steven, Milo, and Harry were all quiet as the Eli imposter continued to strip off his clothes.

"What are you doing?" Harry finally asked.

"Well, my plan is not without a few faults." He pulled off the last of his clothes and dug through another duffel bag for some more. Women's clothes. "With so many people here, frequent changes are required. And in order for me to take on someone's appearance without raising alarm, frequent outfit changes are also required."

Before any of the men could respond, the man who looked like Eli tore off his right ear and tossed it on the cement floor in the corner.

Milo gagged, but Steven was simply dumbfounded.

Next came the other ear. Then the man hooked a finger in his lip and yanked. Surprisingly, there was no blood. It was as if his skin were putty that could be pulled off without pain. He kept going, ripping at his flesh, peeling it off like a snake shedding its skin.

"I'm gonna puke," Milo muttered, but the rest of them ignored him.

Once the layer of skin was piled on the floor, all that was left was an androgynous figure whose skin looked smooth and waxy, as if it had been damaged beyond repair. The man—or creature, or *thing*—turned away from the captured men, who stared in disbelief.

A moment later, the shiny skin began to bubble and the man shook violently as his form took on a new shape. Smaller, softer, smoother.

Within minutes, the psycho went from looking like Eli Harding to looking like Ruby Harding. The imposter casually reached for the clothes she had pulled out from the bag and began to redress. Faded jeans and a matching denim jacket.

"Now," the pyscho said in a voice that sounded exactly like Ruby's, "I have to attend to my guests. I'll be back later, I'm sure, for another…outfit change."

"Wait!" Steven called out. "Samantha and Kathy are here. They'll figure it out. They'll know something is wrong and find a way to stop you."

Turning quickly, the Ruby imposter brought a knife to Steven's throat that she had pulled out of seemingly nowhere. Her lips turned up in a smile. "The girls are in my grasp. They have no idea what's going on. Soon, they will be my sacrifices. And unless you or your friends here want to join them, I suggest you keep your voices down. Okay?"

Milo began nodding before she even finished speaking. The Ruby imposter looked over at Harry, who also nodded. Steven held his stoic gaze for a moment longer, before he relented and agreed as well.

"Good." She put the knife back in the pocket of her jacket and patted Steven's cheek. She raced up the stairs just as fast as she came down. "I'll see you boys later."

CHAPTER 31

There you are." Samantha emerged into the kitchen just as Ruby Harding was closing the basement door. "I've been looking all over for you. Eli said you were around here somewhere."

"Oh, I was down in the basement," she said. "Thought I heard a water leak."

"I hope you didn't find anything." Samantha leaned against the edge of the counter.

"Nope. Dry as a bone down there." Ruby opened the refrigerator. "Do you want anything to drink? I know Eli put some stuff out, but we have extras here. Call it my own little stash."

"Um…I'll take a water, thanks." Samantha glanced back at

the basement door and said, "You know, Steven said he might've had a water leak too. Which is weird because it hasn't been excessively rainy lately. We've had a few days, but nothing terrible."

Ruby set a bottle of water on the counter in front of Samantha. "I think it's just that time of year, you know? Things outside are starting to get wetter. Plus, we live in old houses and all."

Samantha opened the bottle and took a sip. "Right." She didn't think Eli or Ruby knew where Steven lived or whether his house was old or new.

Relax, Sam. She was probably just talking in general. Then another thought came to her: *Maybe you could peek into her mind and see—*

"There you are!" Kathy said in the doorway. "Oh, and Ruby! How are you?"

Their neighbor smiled and leaned against the counter by the sink. "I'm doing well. Just working on getting this house up to snuff."

"Well, the place looks great," Kathy said. "You guys must've done a lot of work. I haven't been in here in—" She looked over at her sister. "What has it been? Like five, ten years?"

"Something like that," Samantha murmured, then quickly added, "You know, Ruby, for as much work as you've done, we haven't seen you outside a lot."

Ruby smiled and waved her hand dismissively. "Oh, I'm not

one for colder weather. When we put away the swim trunks, I pull out the blankets and hibernate inside. You probably won't see much of me until spring, honestly."

Kathy laughed. "I know! I feel like I don't go out much anymore, either."

Samantha gave her sister a look. Kathy was always going out for something or another. Sure, maybe her trips to the bar or the club had dwindled, but she was still leaving the house on a regular basis. Unlike Ruby.

"Where'd you leave Eli?" Samantha asked her sister.

"Oh, it was the weirdest thing," Kathy said. "I was talking to him and then he just stopped and walked away mid-sentence."

"While you were in the middle of a conversation?"

Kathy nodded.

"Oh, I'm sure he just remembered he needed to take care of something," Ruby said. "He's always putzing around with something or another. He didn't mean anything by it. He can be kind of spacey."

Kathy nodded. "It was just weird."

"That is the word of the day, isn't it?" Samantha muttered.

"Yeah, where are Steven and Milo?" Kathy turned and looked through the doorway into the growing crowd in the next room. "They were supposed to be here."

"I thought I saw Steven come in," Ruby said.

Samantha turned to her. "But you were in the basement."

"I saw him before I went down there," she said, maintaining

a smile that Samantha didn't think was natural.

"Right."

"All right, Sam," Kathy said. "Let's do another lap around and see if we can find them—or anyone else we know. It was nice talking to you, Ruby!"

"You too!" She waved and smiled wide.

Samantha tried not to stare at Ruby before she followed her sister into the thick of the party, but she had a bad feeling in the pit of her gut that something wasn't right.

CHAPTER 32

Kathy squeezed between several people and found a spot in the corner of the living room that was open enough for her and Samantha to talk. More guests had certainly arrived, making it nearly impossible to move anywhere without accidentally bumping into someone. With open cups containing an assortment of drinks creating obstacles along the way, navigating the maze became more challenging.

Kathy was used to that challenge from the clubs she went to with Trisha, but she could tell by Samantha's look of perpetual annoyance when she broke through the crowd that her sister did not feel the same way.

"These people won't even move!" Samantha said loudly. "Even when they see you're trying to get through."

"Sometimes you have to go around." Kathy shrugged. "Or just push through."

"That's a bit rude. Anyway, we've circled the house twice and haven't seen the guys. Although, in this crowd we may have walked right by them without even realizing it." She stood on her tip-toes and tried to look over everyone's heads for any sign of Steven or Milo, but she couldn't see much.

"I'm sure they'll turn up," Kathy said. "If worse comes to worst, we could wait for them out on the front porch."   "I just thought they'd be here by now. Ruby said they were!" Samantha looked around again on her toes, and then slunk back down and looked at her sister. "This party has got to be against fire safety regulations or something."

"I'm not sure those apply at a house party."

"And what if the cops show up and shut it down?" Samantha worried. "I don't want to get arrested."

Kathy rolled her eyes. "We'll be fine."

Samantha groaned. "Where are they? I'm worried something happened."

"They're just running late."

"Both of them?" Samantha snapped. "Besides, that's not like Steven. He's usually very punctual. And if he's not, he calls."

"Maybe he's calling our house."

"Do you think I should go back and check?"

Kathy laughed. "No! I think you should have a drink and relax!"

"I just have this really bad feeling." Samantha bounced on her feet and continued to look around.

"Bad feeling about what?"

"Well, Steven's been acting weird lately."

"Right. The kissing thing. We've been through this. Just relax."

"But it's more than that. He's been lying. I know for sure."

"How? Did you read his mind?"

Samantha shook her head. "No. I can just tell. And now he doesn't show up when he says he's going to? It's not like him."

"So what do you think happened to him?"

"I don't know. Maybe somehow, some creature found out that he knows about us and is going after him."

"Without you knowing?" Kathy asked. "It doesn't seem likely. Besides, how do you explain Milo having his odd moments too? Or even Eli and Ruby. They seem off too. Then again, I try not to have prolonged conversations with Eli…"

"I don't know," Samantha repeated. "I just don't like it."

"I think it's just a full moon thing," Kathy said. "In a couple days, it'll pass."

"I see him!" Samantha raised her hand high above her head and waved.

Kathy stared, thinking to herself that Samantha was the one who seemed off. Not herself. Perhaps that was just the paranoia creeping through her about Steven.

When Steven finally joined their corner, Samantha wrapped

him in a hug and he took that as his cue to maul her. Kathy stood by awkwardly as her older sister made out with her boyfriend. She tried to find somewhere to divert her eyes, but there wasn't much to look at in the corner.

Kathy never felt so much like the third wheel than she did at that moment.

Finally, Samantha pulled away. "Where the hell have you been?"

"Time got away from me," Steven said. "Sorry. I've been here for a little while, looking around for you."

"Hmm, just like Ruby said," Kathy murmured.

Samantha ignored her. "Funny, we've been looking for you."

Steven smiled and wiggled his eyebrows. "I could tell you missed me by that kiss."

Samantha took half a step back from him—all that she could in the small space they had claimed as theirs—and pointed her finger at him. "You *know* I don't like to be *that* couple that's always making out. So stop trying to clean out my throat with your tongue!"

Kathy made a face.

"I just can't help myself." Steven reached for Samantha, but Kathy stopped him.

"Have you seen Milo?" she asked. "I haven't been able to find him, either."

"I think he was in line for the bathroom," Steven said.

"Where's that?" Kathy asked.

"Down the hall, toward the back door," he said. "The line is pretty long."

Kathy smiled. "No problem, I just want to talk to him."

"I think I remember there being a bathroom upstairs too," Samantha said. "I'm sure Eli and Ruby wouldn't mind if—"

"No," Steven snapped. "Upstairs is off-limits. Eli told me that when I came in."

Kathy looked to Samantha, who had the same confused expression as she did.

"Eli didn't say anything like that to us," Samantha said.

"I'm sure he meant to. Just stay down here."

Sensing a spat was about to erupt, Kathy announced that she was going to find Milo and began to push her way through the crowd.

CHAPTER 33

By the time Kathy worked her way to the hallway, she saw the line for the bathroom stretched the length of the wall beside the ornate staircase and around the bottom step into the dining room. People cluttered the space, holding drinks, chatting, and fixing their outfits in the hallway mirror.

No sign of Milo, though.

She pushed around a few people and lifted to her toes to try to spot him, but she couldn't see him anywhere.

Maybe he's in the bathroom now, she thought.

Taking cover in a spot near the doorway to the kitchen, Kathy watched the end of the hallway, hoping that Milo would emerge from inside the powder room.

"Do you want a drink?"

Kathy nearly jumped when she felt someone reach for her arm. She turned and saw it was Milo, who stood just inside the kitchen with a red plastic cup in his hand.

"Sorry," he said with a smirk. "There's no line for the drinks in here."

She stepped into the kitchen to get away from the crowd—and the noise—so the two of them could have a conversation without shouting.

As she turned up to look at him, he pressed her against the wall and kissed her. His free hand slid around to her back and pushed her closer to him. When he pulled away, she took a moment to catch her breath.

That was certainly another level of their relationship that they hadn't explored yet. Not since the club, at least.

"Where have you been?" Milo sipped his cup with one hand while the other sat possessively on her hip.

"Waiting for you," she said, still breathless. "When did you get here?"

"A while ago. Been looking all over for you."

She narrowed her eyes, Samantha's paranoia seeping into her own mind. "So have I."

He smirked. "We must've just missed each other."

"I thought you would've met me at my house."

"I planned on it," he said. "But by time I got here, your house looked dark, so I just came right here."

"Right." Kathy looked over Milo's shoulder and saw a small

group of people talking near the doorway to the living room, but there was no one else in the kitchen.

Milo followed her gaze and looked over his shoulder. "What is it?"

"My neighbor—or one of them—she was just in here," Kathy said.

"The woman?"

She nodded. "Yeah."

"I think I saw her go off into the living room. Maybe she's refilling the drinks in the cooler."

"Maybe."

"Kathy!" Samantha pushed through the crowd from the living room and met them in the kitchen. "Milo, there you are. At least now we know they're both here."

"Where's Steven?" Kathy asked.

Samantha shrugged. "He disappeared on me."

"You lost him?" Milo chuckled.

"He said he was going to get me a drink, but that was a while ago," Samantha said. "I went to go look for him and couldn't find him."

Kathy crossed the room to peek into the living room. "I'm sure you just bypassed each other without even realizing it."

"Hey, did you guys see that painting in the dining room?" Milo pointed with his cup toward the opposite entry to the kitchen.

Both sisters looked at him with confusion.

"It's beautiful," he went on. "I'm sure you'd love it."

"That's nice," Samantha said, "but right now I'm more concerned with finding Steven."

"He's a grown man, it's not like you need to keep tabs on him," Milo said. "And it's a party! Where's he going to go?"

Kathy nodded. "He's got a point."

"I'm serious, though," he went on. "This painting is awesome. I'd love to know what you guys think of it. Come on." He waved them forward.

"Since when do you like art?" Kathy walked back through the doorway to the hall, Samantha in tow.

"I've always liked art," he said. "I guess I just haven't told you yet."

He's got me there, she thought. *So far, we've mostly only been talking about me—or maybe that's just all I've cared to remember.*

Both sisters still looked skeptical.

"Look, you're here to relax and have fun, right?" he went on.

"Yeah," Kathy said.

She and Milo both turned to Samantha, who shrugged again.

"Then just go look at the painting," Milo said. "Let me know what you think." He leaned closer to Kathy. "Consider it a test. Deep insight will win you a date with me."

She rolled her eyes with a smirk. "Fine, but only if you mix me a drink while I'm gone. We're here to relax, aren't we?"

Kathy took a step to the door and then reached back and grabbed Samantha's hand.

CHAPTER 34

I really couldn't care less about this painting," Samantha told Kathy once they were out of the kitchen.

She couldn't shake the feeling that something was wrong. This party seemed off. Were there really this many people who knew Eli? Even in addition to the people in their neighborhood, it seemed like a lot. She recognized some, but not all. Then again, that might've said more about how neighborly she was than anything. And half of the people were wearing Halloween costumes, making it harder to tell who was who. Still, it was hard to believe that Eli Harding had befriended this many people so shortly after moving to the street.

"Me neither." Kathy pulled them out of sight of the kitchen

before turning back to her sister. "I think something *is* going on."

Samantha felt relieved. "Oh good."

"Good?"

"It's not just me then. What made you think something's up?"

"Well, for one, we haven't seen Eli since we walked in," Kathy said. "And Ruby disappeared too. Notice how she wasn't in the kitchen?"

Samantha hadn't noticed. She was too wrapped up in where Steven had gone.

"And when I saw Milo, he kissed me—like Steven's been kissing you."

"I told you kisses matter!"

"It's just that Milo and I haven't gotten around to a lot of kissing yet," Kathy explained. "Certainly not like that. It wasn't like him."

"He and Steven both have been acting different," Samantha added.

"Right."

"Do you think they're under a spell?" Samantha wasn't sure what spell would make them kiss their women with burning passion and otherwise leave them acting…off. And Eli and Ruby? They were missing something. It wasn't unusual for both of Samantha and Kathy's boyfriends to be targeted by evil, but how did their neighbors fit into it?

"I don't know." Kathy turned to the staircase. "But Steven didn't want us to go upstairs, so I think that's where we should start looking."

Samantha nodded and started moving through the crowd toward the staircase. She hoped that Milo or Steven or anyone else they suspected to be under a spell didn't see them go up there.

They moved quickly, hurrying to get up the stairs and out of sight before they could be questioned. Once they got to the second level, the music from below reduced to only a steady beat that they could feel through the floors.

The hallway was dark, but Samantha didn't dare turn on a light. At the top of the stairs was a room with a small twin bed and a dresser. It was tidy and looked like it hadn't been used much. The next door led to a small bathroom with a clawfoot tub and a shower curtain wrapped around it. Next was a second bedroom that looked much like the first, only this had a double bed.

From the end of the hallway, Kathy quietly whispered Samantha's name and waved her on. She had turned on the bedroom light, which revealed a large room with a big bed and white carpeting.

"What is it?" Samantha asked quietly when she entered.

Kathy stood at the closet and pointed. Her face showed complete shock.

Inside the closet, piled up on the floor, looked like wet,

melted plastic. Only, that still didn't quite look right.

Samantha crouched down to examine it closer. The substance had hair in some places. Worse, she saw what looked like the faint shape of an ear and the upward pillowing of a nose.

"I think this is skin."

"Gross." Kathy brought a hand to her mouth and turned away. "Whose is it?"

"I don't know. But did you see this?" Samantha pointed to the back of the closet.

Balled up and shoved beside the vat of skin were white sheets, stained red with blood.

"So someone was skinned alive on the bed?" Kathy asked.

Samantha rose to her feet and moved to examine the bed. "There don't seem to be any marks on the headboard from restraints. If someone was skinned alive, they wouldn't just sit back and take it."

"Unless they were killed before." Kathy took her turn kneeling beside the pile of skin. "Or maybe this sheet was used to clean up the mess from somewhere else."

Samantha pulled back the comforter and revealed the naked bed, stripped down to the mattress. "It was definitely here."

"Sam, this looks…familiar."

"What do you mean?"

"I think…I think this might be Eli's skin."

"That's impossible," Samantha said. "We just saw him downstairs, perfectly healthy."

"Did we, though?" Kathy got to her feet, but still couldn't pull her eyes away from the bottom of the closet. "If this is Eli's skin, that means he's probably dead. And if he's dead, then maybe Ruby is too. Maybe even Harry and Milo and…Steven."

Samantha squeezed her eyes shut and held up a hand in Kathy's direction. "Okay, okay. Just wait a minute." All the speculation was making it impossible for her to think straight. "For all we know, this is a regular serial killer."

"And that's supposed to make me feel *better*?" Kathy asked. "We're standing in a crime scene!"

"It makes our job easier," Samantha reasoned. "If this *is* a serial killer, we just need to call the police and they'll take care of it."

"While we panic from across the street? I don't think so. Sam, there is a pile of skin here! That has to be supernatural."

Samantha looked in the closet again. That was hard to explain. As was the fact that everyone seemed to be accounted for, despite the skin indicating otherwise. Kathy was right. This was supernatural in some way. But how?

"Look at this." Kathy stood by the wall near the headboard.

"What is it?" Samantha crossed the room and saw for herself.

Dried blood drip marks ran down the wall behind the headboard. Upon closer inspection, Samantha saw that other marks on the wall had been hastily cleaned up.

"Whether or not this is supernatural," Kathy said, "something bad happened in this room."

CHAPTER 35

W hat do you think we should do?" Kathy asked Samantha with a tense look.

She knew Kathy was scared. So was Samantha, but more because they didn't know very much at all except for the fact that something wasn't right.

Samantha looked from the blood behind the headboard, to the vat of skin in the closet, to the bloodstained sheets. She took it all in, taking inventory and running through several *what-if* scenarios in her head. There was an explanation where all of this made sense.

The pile of skin just wasn't clicking. Nor was the fact that everyone appeared healthy, despite their behaviors.

Finally, Samantha sucked in a big breath and turned back to

her sister. "Okay, the first thing we need to do is identify what exactly we're up against. We can't do anything until we know that and how to stop them. That will hopefully also help us figure out who it is that did this."

Kathy nodded. "Okay. And then what? We can't exactly cast a spell in a house full of people."

"No, we can't." Samantha chewed on the inside of her cheek and looked down the dark hallway. At the end, the music and murmur of multiple conversations radiated up from downstairs. "We'll need to get whoever is responsible for this out of the house—or at least away from everyone else. Having a house full of people is really just asking for problems. They could potentially all be targets."

"They could potentially all be *enemies* too," Kathy added.

"Let's not think like that. We need to protect them and we can't exactly send them all home because whoever is killing people might sneak out with everyone. It would give away the fact that we're on to them." If Steven and Milo and the others weren't already dead, telling the killer that they were exposed would surely be a death sentence to the men in their lives.

"We should at least get Steven and Milo out," Kathy said. "We can't risk them—"

"No, Kathy." Samantha motioned to the closet. "We don't know who's doing this. For all we know, it *could* be Steven or Milo under the influence of a spell. If we let them go—or tell them what we've found out—that could end badly. Until we know for sure what's going on, we can't trust anyone. We need to act like everything's normal."

"So how are we going to find out who's behind this?"

"You run home and look in the book," Samantha said. "Try not to let anyone see you leave."

"You're not coming with me?"

"Someone needs to stay back and keep an eye on things in case the killer tries to take another victim," Samantha said. "In a house full of people, it might just be the perfect cover. Besides, since I'm able to read minds now, maybe I can pick through to try to spot this guy before he strikes again."

"There's a lot of people here. Are you sure you'll be able to read minds without just hearing a lot of noise?"

Samantha considered it. When her specialty first grew, she heard every single thought people around her were having. Since then, she'd been able to tune out the noise, but she still didn't have the best grasp on the power to cherry-pick who she eavesdropped in on.

"I have to try," she said. "It's better than not doing anything."

They turned off the lights in the bedroom and returned downstairs, checking for any sign of Eli, Ruby, Steven, or Milo before merging in with the rest of the crowd. Samantha followed Kathy toward the back door at the end of the hallway by the bathroom. There were fewer people in line and since the party had been going for a while now, many of them were too drunk to pay attention to who was going where.

"Be safe and hurry back," Samantha murmured to Kathy once she got to the door.

The younger sister nodded. "Of course. You be safe too. We have no idea who this guy is or—"

"There you are!" Steven's voice boomed from the end of the hall. He moved around the small crowd in the hallway and met them by the door. "I've been looking all over for you. Milo mentioned that you guys went to check out some painting, but you were gone by time I got there."

"Yeah, we got sidetracked," Samantha said. "Ran into Carol Harris, from down the street."

Steven looked around. "I didn't see her anywhere."

"Oh, maybe she left already."

He looked over and saw Kathy's hand on the doorknob. "Going somewhere?"

As much as the sinister look on his face disgusted Samantha, they needed a distraction. Quickly, she stepped toward him, placed her hands on the sides of his face, pressed him against the wall and kissed him hard. She ignored the stares and the hooting and hollering from the drunk spectators and listened until she heard the back door close.

Kathy had managed to escape.

CHAPTER 36

Kathy's racing heart didn't begin to slow until she made it inside the front door of her house. She didn't dare flick on the lights, fearful that she would somehow be spotted from across the street.

The pile of skin she found in the closet was an image she couldn't get out of her head. What was worse was the worry that followed it: if that happened to Eli, what did that mean about everyone else she and Samantha cared about?

Kathy raced up the stairs to where she kept the magic book under her bed. She held it close to her chest and carried it into the bathroom, where the window looked out onto the backyard. There, she felt safe enough to turn on the light so she could actually see what she was reading.

Taking a seat on the toilet lid, she propped the book in her lap and anxiously flipped through the pages. The trouble was, she didn't know *what* she was looking for, which meant she needed to read each entry carefully to see if any of them fit.

If the killer was hiding in plain sight amongst the crowd, that meant they looked like one of the crowd, which ruled out all the creatures who didn't maintain a human presence like an anguis, imp, or even a banshee.

She stopped on the page for sorcerers and considered if there was one in their midst casting spells on the people at the party, but nobody at the party seemed to be suffering any ill-effects from a spell. Nobody was sleeping off the effects of magic, nor was there any opportunity for a sorcerer to even cast a spell.

And what would be the point? Sorcerers go after power and unless the wool had *seriously* been pulled over her eyes, Kathy was confident that Eli and Ruby weren't magical. And neither of them held major positions of power at work. It didn't make sense.

Kathy kept flipping through the pages and landed on the page for a spirit. It was possible that Eli and Ruby had been possessed, but then who had been killed and left the blood spatter? And that didn't explain the pile of skin in the closet.

Kathy shuddered at the thought. She grasped the page and was about to keep flipping, when the next entry caught her eye: vampire.

While she was confident that a vampire wouldn't waste blood—and there was a lot of it on those sheets—it gave her another idea. Vampires were a form of shapeshifters, but there were beings that simply had the ability to change their shape.

Flipping back a couple pages, she found the entry on shapeshifters and read it to herself.

Shapeshifters are able to change their shape and size at will. Whether it be to morph to look like another person or animal, these creatures are very powerful. With their ever-changing appearance, shapeshifters are nearly impossible to spot with the naked eye unless they are witnessed changing shape.

While shapeshifters are a unique creature in and of themselves, witches, wizards, demons, and other creatures have been known to master the art of shapeshifting, though typically with limited results. A true shapeshifter is able to morph into any living creature, while a witch may only be able to morph into one thing (a cat, for instance).

Rest assured, there are potions and spells that allow others to see the true identity of a shapeshifter.

The trouble was, the book didn't list any of the potions or spells available to see the true form of a shapeshifter. Kathy considered whether a shapeshifter was what they were up against. It was the best option she had found in the book, which of course didn't mean that it was correct. Still, it was the only lead they had. And it explained a lot.

Within the pile of skin, there were features that looked like Eli Harding, even though he was walking around perfectly healthy at the party. And it made sense that the shifter would have to kill Eli before he took his shape, or risk being found out and exposed.

Kathy brought a hand to her mouth as she considered what else that meant: Steven and Milo had been acting strange as well. Were they among the people the shifter was impersonating? And if the shifter had killed Eli to take his shape, what did that mean for Steven and Milo?

She shook her head and closed the book. She couldn't think of worst-case scenarios right now. She needed to do something that would help them stop the shifter before he could hurt anyone else.

Leaving the book on the bathroom vanity, Kathy raced downstairs and went to the kitchen.

Samantha kept a full stock of pre-made potions in the cabinet beside the pantry for any number of uses. Kathy sifted through them, reading the tiny labels to see if any of them would help her see the shapeshifter's true identity. There were potions to ward off evil, to heal, and to tell the truth, but nothing about revealing a true identity.

Kathy closed the cabinet, frustrated.

What else could help us with a shapeshifter? she thought to herself as she leaned on the island.

She thought of what stopped a vampire: a wooden stake through the heart or decapitation. She couldn't imagine chopping someone's head off and neither she nor Samantha were the best at hand-to-hand fighting. Driving a wooden stake into the shifter's heart wouldn't work, either. Especially if they looked like someone the sisters cared about.

Her mind wandered to another type of shapeshifter: werewolves. The lore said that what stopped them was a silver bullet to the heart. Once again, they were fresh out of silver bullets and the gun to fire it with. And that was assuming that that method would even work.

But there were two common themes between those methods: driving something through the shifter's heart. Perhaps if she combined both of them—maybe a silver stake—it would be enough to stop the shifter. They would just have to rely on Samantha's power to figure out who the shifter was.

Snatching a pen and a pad of paper from the counter, Kathy sat at the table and got to work crafting a spell that she hoped would stop the shapeshifter. It had to work because they had no other option.

CHAPTER 37

Samantha pulled away from Steven, but kept her hands on the side of his face for a while. She studied his eyes, trying to determine what was going on with him.

He smiled wide. "What happened to not wanting to broadcast our affection?"

At least that much he remembered.

"Maybe I've had a little too much to drink," she lied. "I'm going to go take a look at that painting. Maybe we'll find Milo. Come on."

She turned and disappeared back into the crowd, trying her best to focus her power on specific people, but the collective noise from all the chatter—and all the thoughts—made it nearly impossible to determine who was thinking or saying what. She still needed to practice this new ability.

Morgan is looking great in that costume.

I shouldn't have drank so much. I have no idea what anyone's talking about.

It's hot in here. Someone should open a window.

Once Samantha got back to the painting, she looked around the room and tried her best to focus her power on one person in particular and read their thoughts. She was able to narrow in on one person with her persuasion, but at the moment, she was struggling to do it with her telepathy. All of the noise from around was breaking her concentration, infiltrating her mind.

Can I drive home tonight?

This costume makes me feel ridiculous.

Whose house is this again?

She felt a dull headache begin to form right at her forehead from all the conversations slipping into her mind.

Too many people in here, she decided. *Better to try somewhere with fewer people.*

Working her way through the crowd, she crossed toward the table with the drinks in the living room, but stumbled as she did. Now that she had invited the thoughts into her head, she was having a hard time deciphering between them all. It was like she couldn't turn off her power. There were too many people to tune out.

Jordan made this drink very strong.

Did Marcie go outside?

SHAPESHIFTER

Hopefully the line for the bathroom has died down.

The headache grew worse and Samantha brought a hand up to her forehead and reached out for the nearest chair. There was a man sitting in it, leaning over and talking to a woman beside him, but Samantha didn't care. She sat on the arm of the chair as her vision began to blur from the pain.

Did the killer cast a spell on me? Or is this purely a side effect of the power I still can't control? Samantha didn't know what to think except for the fact that she wanted to get out of the house. She needed to get away from the crowd and the thoughts and the voices. For every voice she heard through her ears, they were multiplied by the number of foreign thoughts she heard in her head.

What the hell does this chick think she's doing?

Is she going to hurl on us?

Looks like someone can't hold their liquor.

"Hey, are you okay?"

Samantha felt a hand on her shoulder and looked up to see a younger man standing beside her. He looked much younger than the rest of them at the party, but still not completely out of place.

"Drink too much?" he asked.

She shook her head slowly, but immediately winced and reached for her forehead again.

"Come on." He grabbed ahold of her arm to help her up. "Let's get you some water and take you someplace quieter."

Samantha followed him as he led her through the crowd. This was something that Steven would do for her. Take care of her. But, once again, he had mysteriously wandered off. She hoped Kathy was having better luck back home with the magic book.

When they got into the kitchen, the noise from the other rooms was stifled and Samantha could finally hear herself think again. The voices in her head had died down, but her head still ached.

The man stood at the sink and filled a cup of water before passing it off to her. "Drink this. It'll make you feel better."

"Just water?" she asked.

He nodded.

Samantha took a sip, then another, before downing the whole glass. She could feel her head begin to clear, although she knew she wasn't at full strength yet. She still had a long way to go with her power, no matter what she had accomplished with it when she and Kathy faced the valkyries.

"You want more?" he asked.

"No, thank you." She set the cup on the counter and looked around. There wasn't anyone else in the kitchen, which was nice to keep the volume down. But where had Steven disappeared to? After the kiss she gave him, she thought he would be following her around like a puppy-dog.

The man came around the island and stood beside her. "Feeling better?" He angled his eyes to meet hers.

"A little, thanks."

"Don't mention it." He stacked her cup among the other plastic cups on the island in an effort to clean up. Nearly every surface of the counter had something on it: cups, napkins, liquor bottles, pizza boxes, styrofoam plates.

The man extended his hand. "I'm Harry."

"Samantha." Her eyes narrowed. "Do you know my sister, Kathy?"

"Oh yeah! From English class!" Her gripped her hand tight.

She rubbed her forehead, her memory slow amidst the subsiding pain. "I'm sorry, but aren't you supposed to be missing? Kathy said you weren't in class yesterday and your parents are worried sick."

Harry's smile faded and he gripped her hand tighter.

It's him! Samantha thought to herself. *That explains why his parents said he disappeared even though Kathy still saw him earlier this week!*

Roughly, Harry pulled her closer to him. She pushed away to free herself with her other hand, but he held tight.

"Help!" she shouted, but her plea disappeared into the noise of the crowd. The next moment, she felt a rag over her mouth. As much as she knew she shouldn't breathe it in, her panic took over and soon her headache was no longer a problem.

CHAPTER 38

We need a plan to get out of here," Milo said. "We can't just sit here and pass up the opportunity of a houseful of people directly above us!"

After seeing the psycho creature coming and going several times throughout the course of the night, Milo had somehow gained a sense of confidence. Steven figured it was from the fact that it looked like the psycho really wasn't going to kill them.

"He said if we call for help he'll kill us and the girls," Steven reminded him. "That's not something I'm willing to risk."

"All I know is that if I have to watch that weirdo peel off another layer of skin, I really am going to puke," Harry said from the other side of Steven.

The pyscho had been running in and out of the basement all

day to morph into different people. Usually Steven or Milo, but he'd also changed into Eli, Ruby, and even Harry.

"Never mind the fact that every time he changes into one of us, he's flashing the goods out for everyone to see," Harry added.

"Embarrassed, are we?" Milo stretched to look around Steven at Harry.

"Modest, is more like it," Harry corrected.

"Sure," Milo added. "You just don't want anyone looking at your little—"

"Both of you, be quiet," Steven said firmly. "It's bad enough we're tied up here helpless, I don't want to have to also listen to you two compare sizes."

"That's why I'm saying we need to come up with a plan to get out of here!" Milo said.

"Apparently his fiancée can get us out," Harry said.

"Samantha? What's she going to do?"

"Just trust me," Steven said.

"Oh, like we trusted you when you said that this creep really was going to let us go?" Milo asked. "He's going to kill us!" He turned toward the stairs and shouted, "Help! Somebody! We're trapped in the basement!"

"Would you knock it off!" Steven hissed.

"Yeah, you're annoying as hell," Harry said.

"If it'll get us out—"

The basement door swung open and slammed against the wall. Heavy footsteps came down the stairs, followed by a series of thuds. It was a sound Steven had heard before when the psycho brought down Milo.

He had yet another prisoner.

As the psycho—who currently looked like Harry—came into view, Steven's heart sunk when he saw who he was carrying. Laying limply in his arms was Samantha in a beautiful black dress that Steven knew she was likely a little self-conscious about.

Seeing the creature manhandle her like that summoned a rage in Steven he didn't know existed.

"Sam!" he called to her, even though he knew she wouldn't answer.

Harry looked over to Steven. "Wait, *this* is the girl who is supposed to save us?"

CHAPTER 39

Kathy had to push her way through the door when she returned to Eli and Ruby's house. There were a lot more people in the crowd now. Many of them drunk, some of them wearing costumes. Some people even loitered on the lawn and in the driveway since the house was so full. The fall breeze brought a chill to Kathy, but for people who'd had a few drinks in them, they probably didn't notice the temperature.

Inside, Kathy fought her way through the thick of the crowd in search of Samantha. She made two trips around the house, increasing her search to include Steven, Milo, Eli, anyone she recognized who could help her get a sense of what happened while she was gone.

Nobody was around.

She regretted taking so long back at the house and wondered if the shifter had gotten to Samantha while she was gone. In hindsight, she thought they should've come up with a codeword to check in with each other, but when Kathy left, they didn't realize they were up against a shapeshifter.

In the hallway, Kathy looked up the stairs. Had Samantha returned to what they found in the bedroom to investigate further?

Kathy took two steps up the stairs before she heard her name called.

Samantha walked up the hallway from the bathroom and motioned into the kitchen. Kathy followed her sister in and welcomed the somewhat quiet of the room.

Once again, nobody else was in the kitchen, opting instead to gather in the more spacious living room. Kathy found that odd since most house parties she'd been to, the kitchen was a focal point being the place where everyone came for drinks or food. Either way, she was too happy about finding her sister to give it too much thought.

Immediately, she wrapped her arms around Samantha and squeezed her tight. "I'm so glad I found you!"

Samantha patted her back and then pulled away. "Relax, Kathy. I wasn't in the bathroom that long."

"Okay, so I think what we're looking at is a shapeshifter."

Samantha's eyebrows went up. "A shapeshifter?"

"Yeah and even though the book said there were potions

and spells out there to allow you to see his true identity, I couldn't find one."

"Huh."

"But then I was thinking about other types of shapeshifters—vampires and werewolves—and I think a silver stake to the heart would kill him."

"A silver stake?"

"I know. Where would we get one of those? So I came up with a spell that I think will work. Now we just need to find him."

"Okay then."

"Okay?" Kathy's eyebrows drew together. "That's all you have to say about it?"

Samantha shrugged. "It sounds like you've got it all covered."

"Except, it doesn't solve another problem we have: we still have no idea where the hostages are. If there are any hostages to be found."

Her sister picked at the pepperoni from one of the pizza boxes. "They'll turn up."

Kathy studied her sister, surprised at the reaction. Something was wrong. She picked at the blouse Samantha was wearing, which looked familiar. "Why did you change? You looked great."

"Oh, someone spilled a drink on me so Ruby lent me some clothes."

"So you did see her?"

"Yeah, why wouldn't I?"

"Well, we couldn't find her and—" Kathy stopped herself. Samantha had been paranoid when Kathy left and now she was entirely casual. And the change of clothes? This had to mean one thing: the shifter had gotten to her while Kathy was gone.

She looked up just in time to see Samantha bring a rag up to her mouth. Kathy swatted it away and stood back, but Samantha charged at her. Raising her hands, Kathy froze time, stopping Samantha in her tracks and bringing a silence to the party.

The temporary escape from the noise brought Kathy some clarity. This definitely wasn't her sister. She should've noticed with the clothes and the fact that Samantha didn't seem to be engaging in the conversation about the shifter. She only hoped that Samantha was still alive and being held somewhere with Steven, Milo, and everyone else the shifter had hopefully only captured.

Taking another step back from the imposter, Kathy called out her sister's name. Her time freeze only worked on the party. It didn't have an effect on the people outside or downstairs or upstairs. If Samantha was stashed somewhere, now was the time to find her.

If she hadn't been knocked unconscious.

"Samantha!" Kathy cried out again.

"Down here!"

She turned to the basement door at the sound of a man's

voice. Once again, it was familiar, but she couldn't place it with everything else running through her mind.

Pushing open the door, she stepped onto the landing and descended the stairs.

CHAPTER 40

In the basement, Kathy looked down the line at Harry, Steven, Milo, and Samantha. All four of them had their hands tied to the rafter above their heads. They all looked terrible—especially Harry. The guys were all sweaty and dirty, but he looked the worst. Almost thin, like he'd been here the longest.

"Kathy!" Steven cried out. "There's this freak who peels off his skin and he says you and Samantha are going to be his first sacrifices!"

Kathy rushed to Samantha and began to untie her. Her older sister was still woozy, leaning heavily on her restraints to keep her standing. Kathy wasn't sure the spell to kill the shifter would be powerful enough with just one witch. Samantha needed to wake up.

"Kathy, I didn't believe that you'd be able to save us," Milo said. "I didn't think you had anything to do with any of this. I must be dreaming. This is just stuff that happens in movies, right?"

She ignored him as she worked on freeing her sister. Finally, she loosened the slack around the rafter and Samantha sunk heavily into her arms.

"Sam, sweetie, come on," Kathy told her. She gently slapped her face to try to revive her more. "Wake up. We need both of us to say the spell."

"The spell?" Milo asked. "What are you talking about?"

"Not now," Kathy snapped at him.

"Leave her," Steven told Kathy. "Help get us down. The more of us who are free, the better. We should be able to overpower him."

Judging by the haggard looks on all of their faces, Kathy doubted they would be able to stand, let alone last long in a fight against the shifter. Still, she slowly set Samantha down on the concrete and leaned her against a post. She took one step toward Steven and hesitated.

What if there was more than one shifter? How did she know this was really Steven, Milo, and Harry?

She shook her head and stepped forward to free Steven. The shifter expected to bring her down here to join the rest of the hostages. She got the jump on him. It served the shifter no purpose to tie up his ally in the basement as well.

"Where is he?" Harry asked. "Why did it get quiet upstairs?"

"It's only temporary," Kathy murmured as she fussed with the ropes around the rafters. Steven had been hanging here longer, so the knots had more time to tighten under his weight.

"So how long do we have before he comes back?" Milo asked. "Or are we going to end up in the freezer too?"

"Knock it off!" Steven called out. He shifted on his tiptoes to do his best to help loosen the slack, but Kathy's fingers were sore from freeing Samantha's binds and the knots were impossible.

As she worked, she couldn't help but notice that there were several other piles of skin around the basement, most of them grouped around several duffel bags on the floor beside two large freezers against the wall. The basement must've been a frequent stop for him to change shape.

Kathy jumped when the noise above them erupted again.

"He's coming," she murmured with a tremble. Their lives all depended on her.

As if on cue, the Samantha imposter bounded down the stairs in a hurry. Kathy gave up on Steven's restraints and stood protectively in front of him.

But the shifter didn't charge at Kathy. He immediately went to Samantha, holding her against his body, which looked just like her.

Kathy took a step toward her sister, but stopped when she

saw the glimmer of the knife appear at Samantha's throat.

"Don't!" she shouted.

"Freeze him!" Steven told Kathy. "Don't let him hurt her!"

She locked eyes with the shifter. "Please, don't hurt her."

"Then lay down on the floor with your hands where I can see them," the shifter said. "Don't try anything!"

Kathy started to crouch to the floor and got to her knees with her hands raised out beside her head. "Let's just talk this over. I don't know what we did to upset you."

"It's not just you. It's all witches!"

"You just don't like witches?" she asked. "Then why tie up these guys?"

"They're collateral," the shifter said. "A way to get to you and your sister."

"But we didn't do anything to you!"

"How do you think I became this monster?" he barked in Samantha's voice. "I was cursed with a poison by a witch who had the audacity to call it a *treatment*. She wanted to celebrate my new *gift*!"

"A witch gave you your powers?" Kathy asked. That was in contrast to what she had just read in the magic book, but maybe this shapeshifter was the anomaly.

The shifter chuckled. "Of course you would call it power. Was it power your felt when you set my apartment on fire?"

"Me? I didn't set anything on fire!"

"You're the only witches I've encountered so far with

enough power! It was a magical fire that deformed me. Made me into a freak. Made me desperate enough to seek out the *help* of a witch."

"I'm sorry that that happened to you, but killing us is not going to change things," Kathy said.

The shifter pressed the knife against Samantha's throat and a small trickle of blood dribbled down. Kathy could see her sister was alert now, very aware of the situation, but unable to speak with the knife so close to her throat.

"You know, the one thing I've learned is that all witches are the same," the shifter said. "You claim to be protectors, but you're really just causing more suffering."

"You were the one who entered our lives," Kathy said. "We didn't know you existed until today."

The fake Samantha laughed. "Yes, I've fooled you for a few days now, haven't I? Even shared a bed with this one here. And had you alone a few times. Could've killed you several times over."

"So why didn't you?"

"I need to find the witches who set my house on fire. The ones who set me on this journey of misery."

"Misery? You seem to be the one in control right now. Your powers—"

"Are not a *gift!*" he barked. "You think living in someone else's life for a moment is something to be cherished? Sure, I've found a way to exist between life and death. Contract a deadly disease? Simply morph into someone who doesn't have it! Feel yourself get older? Take the form of someone younger! I'm immortal."

"So you're going to dedicate your life to killing witches until you happen to find the one who meant to harm you?" Kathy asked. "You want to commit a genocide?"

"If that's what it takes! Your sacrifice will only add to *my* power!"

Kathy noted there was more blood trickling down Samantha's throat and she realized she needed to back off. "Okay, okay. Just take it easy."

"Kathy," Samantha murmured. Kathy shook her head, pleading with her sister not to try anything. Not when she was in such a vulnerable position.

"Get on the floor!" the shifter demanded. "On the floor and don't do anything while I tie you up!"

Kathy moved her hands to the back of her head and slowly lowered herself onto her stomach on the floor. It wasn't long before she felt Samantha's soft hands pulling Kathy's arms down behind her back and looping a rope around them. Kathy turned her face so her cheek rested against the cold concrete. She made eye contact with Steven, communicating without a word that she was sorry she couldn't save them.

Steven, however, was not ready to roll over. He gripped the rafter above him, swung his feet outward, and kicked the shifter in the back as he was bent over Kathy, knocking him to the floor.

"Go!" he shouted.

Kathy shot to her feet and ran to Samantha's side—the *real* Samantha. From the top of her dress, she pulled out the spell she had written back at the house and together the sisters recited:

You're a master of disguise.
You leave heartache in your wake.
You have ended many lives.
Now it's time to seal your fate!

Of all the methods and ways,
that you have torn lives apart.
Nothing will more make you pay,
then a silver stake to your heart!

With a burst of light, a metallic bar formed in the air in front of the sisters and shot like a bullet toward the shapeshifter, striking him directly in the chest. The wound burst with light that filled the space as he cried out in pain. The skin covering Samantha's imposter began to ooze off of the creature, dripping onto the concrete until there was nothing left but a skeleton that collapsed in the pile of skin.

"That's disgusting!" Milo cried out.

Harry, meanwhile, leaned over and vomited on the floor.

Steven ignored both of them and looked to Samantha. "Are you okay?"

SHAPESHIFTER

She nodded weakly and sat back against the post to rest. "So much for being immortal."

Kathy jumped to her feet and hurried to free Steven.

As she worked, Steven breathed out a heavy sigh of relief. "Watching someone who looked like my future wife die like that is not an image I will ever get out of my head."

CHAPTER 41

Kathy pulled her sweater tighter around her as she sat on the front porch beside Samantha. They watched as all the kids traveled up and down the streets in their neighborhood, each of them were dressed in varying degrees of costumes. Some were accompanied by parents, others traveled in groups. Every single one of them had a bag full of candy, though.

"We might run out." Samantha shook the jack-o-lantern bucket she held the treats in.

"Well, if you didn't give handfuls away to every kid who comes up, we'd be fine."

"But they're so cute! Look, here's a little fairy princess and a ninja." She nodded to two kids walking up the path nervously. They held out their bags and Samantha shoveled candy in. "You two are adorable!" She looked up at their parents standing back on the sidewalk and waved with a smile.

The princess and the ninja thanked them, then turned and walked back up the path.

"You might need to run to the store," Samantha said.

"Seriously, it's called *rationing*, Sam!" Kathy's smile faded when she saw the next person walking down the sidewalk toward them: Milo. He wore a dark jacket over a white T-shirt tucked into his jeans. Clean, rested, and quite different from the last time Kathy had seen him.

"Looks like you have your own trick-or-treater," Samantha told her. "Have you talked to him at all since it happened?"

"Not to him or Harry," she muttered.

Harry hadn't been in class that morning when she went, which she expected. His parents were probably unlikely to let him out of their sight anytime soon.

What she hadn't been expecting was Roger telling her that Harry had dropped the course. She couldn't blame him after what he'd gone through. She just hoped he kept his promise and didn't tell anyone they were witches.

As Milo approached with a somber look, she hoped he would do the same.

"Hey." He offered a tight smile to both sisters.

"Hi," Samantha replied.

He raised his eyebrows to Kathy. "Can we talk?"

Kathy nodded and got to her feet. "Sure, let's go inside."

Once they got through the door, Kathy rubbed her arms and embraced the heat of the house. They stood in the foyer because she could tell he didn't want to stay long.

"I've been doing a lot of thinking." Milo studied his hands, fidgeting. "What happened across the street…" He let out a deep breath. "It's going to take me a while to get through that. If I ever do."

Kathy nodded. "Of course. It was very traumatic for you. I can't imagine what you went through." She thought back to the only other time she'd been captured: with the valkyries in Valhalla. But that was different. She had experienced events similar to that before. What happened to Milo was so far out of his realm of reality.

"So while I work through that, I don't think we'll be able to see each other anymore." He finally met her eyes. In his own, all Kathy saw was pain. "Don't worry, I'll keep your secret. After all, you saved me."

Seeing the torment displayed on Milo's face, Kathy wished she would've noticed the shifter sooner. She wondered how many times she'd been with the shifter thinking it was Milo. How many kisses they'd exchanged. The thought made her skin crawl. And it wasn't like she could ask Milo, either. That point was trivial when put up against his capture.

"It's just that seeing you would remind me of what happened," he went on. "And I want to get to a place where I don't always think about it. I'm losing sleep. My focus is all off at work. Even coming here is hard, being right across the street and all. That's why it took me a couple days to get over here."

Kathy nodded, feeling sadder than she thought she would. She wasn't in love with Milo and she certainly knew this day was coming, but now that it was here, it was harder to take than she thought. Perhaps it was because she had her own reminders of that night, like the police tape that was now spread across the front door of the Harding house. She saw it every time she stepped outside.

"I'm sorry," he murmured, avoiding her eyes again.

"No, don't be." She reached out and rubbed his arm. "You need to take care of yourself first and foremost. Take however long you need to work through this."

Milo swallowed hard. "That's the thing. I'm not sure I'll ever be able to see you or come to this neighborhood without thinking about what happened."

Kathy nodded as she realized this was a permanent thing. She forced a smile for his benefit. "That's okay. I understand."

He looked at her and frowned. "I'm sorry. I wish I could, but—"

She felt tears welling up in her own eyes and swatted in the air to pass off his comments. "Milo, don't worry about me. I'm a big girl. I can handle it. I've dealt with this kind of witchy thing before and I will again. I just want to make sure you're okay."

"Thanks." He leaned over and hugged her.

She squeezed him tight, savoring the moment she knew she would never experience again. "Take care of yourself. And call me if you ever need anything."

He pulled away and sniffled, doing his best to straighten his face so nobody knew he'd been crying.

"I'll miss you, Kathy," he said. "Please, be safe."

"I will. And I'll miss you too. I just want you to get better."

He nodded again and stepped out the door. Kathy followed him out and took a seat beside her sister as she passed out candy to a pirate and Beetlejuice.

When the kids walked back up the path to rejoin their friends, Samantha turned to Kathy and asked, "Well?"

"It's over," she said with a sigh.

"Are you okay?"

Kathy shrugged. "It never feels good to get broken up with, but I guess I'm not heartbroken. Still hurts."

Samantha slung her arm over Kathy's shoulder. "Yeah."

"If anything, it kind of feels like a relief," she admitted.

"How so?"

"I'm free from having to live up to yet another expectation of me: the girlfriend," Kathy explained. "No matter how much Milo tried to take that pressure off, I could tell it was still there. Like I wasn't doing enough."

"With the right guy, you won't feel that pressure," Samantha said. "And like I said, maybe you just need to be single right now. You're doing a lot."

"Yeah," Kathy said with a sigh again. "Dating is just a lot of fun."

Samantha laughed. "I don't think the guys would always agree. Unless they're into the occasional threat on their life."

Kathy rolled her eyes. "How's Steven doing? That was the first time *he* was in danger since finding out you're a witch."

"Oh, he's a trouper," she said. "Apparently he was trying to build morale while they were down there. Take charge and all that."

"Well, he got Milo and Harry through it, so that's something."

"Yeah. I can tell it still bothers him, though," Samantha said. "It's only natural."

"He's human. The fact that we're not more shook up by it makes *us* the freaks."

Samantha smirked. "In more ways than one."

A breeze came through, rattling dry leaves across the yard. The crowd of kids was thinning, but Kathy knew they'd still get a few more stranglers. As long as no one tried to egg their house. It probably didn't hurt that Samantha was giving out handfuls of candy.

"Where's Steven now?" Kathy asked.

"At his mother's, trying to apologize for snapping at her at the bakery. Apparently that was the shifter."

"Makes you wonder how long the shifter was in our house or alone with us," Kathy said. "He said a couple days, but it's hard to know since we didn't suspect anything."

"Yeah, well, the one thing the shifter did that worked in our favor was create an opportunity for Steven to talk to his mother about boundaries when it comes to planning the wedding and…beyond."

"Are you getting nervous about it? The wedding? It's less than three months away and there's still a lot to do."

Samantha nodded. "We'll pull it off. I'm not terribly picky about the specifics of the wedding. With everything we've dealt with over the last few months I've realized that all I need is him to be happy."

"That's sweet," Kathy said. "And that explains why you were the first to notice that something was off when the shifter was impersonating Steven. You knew that wasn't the man you loved."

"Yeah, but I've been thinking. Since when do shapeshifters peel off their skin?"

Kathy shrugged. "Who knows? He said he got his powers from a witch's potion. So he must not have been a full shifter. The shifting process was slower for him, more painful. He still died like a shifter, though."

"True."

Another group of kids turned onto the pathway leading to their front porch. Two girls were dressed like stereotypical witches with a pointed hat and a broomstick. They were with a boy who was dressed like a cowboy, his boots clicking on the sidewalk with each step.

Kathy reached for a handful of candy in the jack-o-lantern Samantha held. "You wanna know the best thing about Halloween?"

"What's that?" Samantha fished for her own handful.

"There's no such thing as shapeshifter costumes."

Samantha and Steven's wedding day has finally arrived! As the bride and groom and their wedding party prepare for the big day, Talia, the officiant of the wedding who is a witch herself, collapses and is taken to the hospital.

Seeing her sister begin to panic that her wedding is falling apart, Kathy uses magic to find another officiant—but her spell summons Augustus, a sorcerer who has his own agenda. Unbeknownst to Kathy, she wasn't alone when she cast the spell, which gives Steven's mother the ammunition she's been looking for to put a stop to the wedding.

While the sisters are preoccupied with preparing for the big day, a news reporter shows up and catches the use of magic on camera. With the wedding day effectively ruined, Samantha and Kathy must figure out how to put their secret back in the bottle. To make matters worse, Augustus disappears and all the signs point to Talia's collapse being connected to his arrival.

In order to stop Augustus and keep their secret, Samantha and Kathy must rely on help from others, which seems impossible to do when their home is surrounded by news reporters.

Sorcerer is the fifth book in the Coven series, which serves as a prequel series to the Under the Moon series.

SORCERER

COVEN: BOOK 5

Read on for an excerpt of the next book in
the Coven series!

DAVID NETH

CHAPTER 1

reshly fallen snow covered the wooded landscape, untouched by mankind after the previous night's snowfall. In the Allegheny National Forest, there were very few people around to even disturb anything, especially so early in the morning.

But a sudden burst of bright light followed by a loud crack changed all of that as Ezra appeared. His hardy boots landed heavy in the snow. He pulled his fur coat tighter around himself and took only a fraction of a second to take in his surroundings before running off amidst the trees.

A moment later, another burst of light and an equally deafening crack sounded and Augustus appeared. Under the brim of his knit hat, his eyes darted through the early dawn darkness before he spotted his brother. Despite the many layers he was wearing and the freshly fallen snow, his pursuit of Ezra wasn't impaired.

"You run, baby brother, because you know you aren't strong enough to face me," Augustus grunted as he continued the chase.

He raced through the leafless trees, dodging downed logs, boulders, and frozen puddles. As he approached a slope, he shifted his body weight and slid down the snow. He took a heavy step once he reached the bottom and continued running. He only stopped when a long wooden staff extended from behind a tree and crashed into his skull, knocking him to the ground.

The being he had been chasing faded out with a burst of light and Ezra stepped into view.

Astral projection.

"Work smarter, not harder," he said.

Grunting, Augustus got to his feet and pointed his own wooden staff at Ezra, sending a streak of lightning soaring through the air toward him. Ezra rocked his shoulder back as he took the hit, firing his own burst of energy at Augustus.

The two traded attacks with one another, ducking behind trees and diving to the snow to avoid hits. Augustus, however, was more skilled. While Ezra took more time to summon stronger attacks, Augustus muttered ancient spells to himself to empower his own magic, creating a force field around his brother that sent Ezra's magic ricocheting back to him and knocking him to the ground.

Augustus approached and kicked away Ezra's staff—the channel for his magic—and stepped on his brother's chest.

"Where's the book, Ezra?"

Despite being overpowered, the younger brother smiled. "You may have stolen more powers, but without the book, you will never be as powerful as me."

Augustus pressed his boot harder against Ezra's chest. "Unless you're able to read the spells from the book, you're not so powerful yourself."

"But if you kill me, you'll never know where our family grimoire is."

"You stole it!" Augustus bellowed. "Tradition says that it goes to the oldest son, which you are not!"

Ezra smiled wide. "Oldest, no. But smartest, perhaps."

"Where is the book!"

Laughing, Ezra said, "I've hidden it so well that you will never find it. Killing me will make sure of it. And I know you're considering it, despite growing up side-by-side as best *friends*. After all, if I were in your shoes, that's what I would do."

Augustus rested his staff on Ezra's throat. "One last chance, brother. Where is the book?"

Ezra looked down and Augustus turned briefly to see who might've followed them. The distraction was enough for Ezra to grab ahold of the end of Augustus's staff and jam it up into his face when he turned back.

Sorcerer

Ezra rolled across the snow and reached for his staff. It had landed between a fallen log and a boulder, wedged in just right so he couldn't reach it from his position on the ground.

Meanwhile, Augustus raised his staff above him and swirled it in the air. The wind picked up and the morning sky grew even darker as supernatural clouds rolled in. Soon, thunder followed. Waving the staff in Ezra's direction, Augustus summoned a bolt of lightning that struck down from the sky and connected directly with Ezra's chest.

Augustus watched as his brother's body lurched forward from the shock, then slammed back down onto the frozen ground. The clouds began to roll away as smoke wafted off of Ezra's charred, lifeless body.

Expectantly, Augustus extended his hand palm-out toward his brother's body. Slowly, a dim light extended from his palm to Ezra's heart as several sparks of light traveled from the corpse to Augustus.

When the transfer was complete, Augustus closed his palm and his eyes as he breathed in the addition of new powers. He might not have the family grimoire, but he had gained something from the outing. Even if he had to sacrifice his brother as collateral damage.

CHAPTER 2

Samantha's heart continued to race as she stepped into the Belle Valley Fire Hall. After all of their planning and preparation, she was less than twenty-four hours away from getting married.

And the lengthy to-do list weighed heavy on her mind.

Kathy and Steven laid out the tablecloths over the circular tables they had set up. Steven's mother, Mary, set out the small green tealight candles on each table, adorned with small solomon's seal flowers. The green candles represented love and solomon's seal root was used in hand fasting rituals, so Samantha thought a few of its flowers on the table would only help to give their marriage a little extra magical *oomph*.

Steven's father, Marty, and Steven's best man, Robert, were

pulling the round tables off the cart and setting them up for tomorrow's festivities.

"Nervous?" Talia asked Samantha.

Much to Mary's displeasure, Talia was going to be the officiant of the wedding. She sported black hair decorated with white beads, an assortment of rings on her fingers, three talismans hanging from her neck, and ripped black jeans under a faded green blouse that just barely covered the several tattoos along her arms.

Samantha and Kathy had found her at one of the herbal shops they frequented for their potion supplies. They hadn't confirmed that she was a witch too, but there was a definite possibility. There was an unspoken understanding between the sisters and Talia: they all recognized they were witches without verbally acknowledging it.

Samantha didn't mind whether or not Talia was a witch. She was more curious that the ceremony would be official, both legally and spiritually. Turns out Talia had it all covered.

Ever since Samantha introduced her as the officiant, Mary had been keeping her distance. Samantha assumed Marty or Steven had talked to her about it and told her to bite her tongue. It was too close to the wedding to cause waves and, if Samantha was being honest, she was smug about the fact that Samantha had come out triumphant with the wedding venue, among the other plans. While Samantha and Steven listened to Mary's input, they had the ultimate say about all of the arrangements.

And they didn't want much.

"Stressed is more like it," Samantha replied.

"These are all details," Talia assured her. "You've already done the hard part: finding someone to spend the rest of your life with."

Samantha sucked in a deep breath and let it out slowly. She'd been doing that more and more as a way to calm her nerves. "I know, but details are important too."

"To a degree. Is there anything else you want to go over about tomorrow?"

"No, it's not going to be that big of a crowd," Samantha said. "Steven really wants to do the whole, not-see-each-other-before-the-wedding thing." She rolled her eyes. "I guess I've planned everything else, so he can have that. We just have to make sure we're separated tomorrow."

"Steven told me he was arriving early tomorrow with his one lone groomsman," Talia said. "What time do you think you'll be arriving?"

Samantha looked over at Robert. Steven had wanted to invite a couple more of his friends from college. He'd been in their weddings, so it was assumed that they'd be in his too. But Samantha really only wanted Kathy standing up beside her. She didn't have too many other close girlfriends, so Steven decided to have only a best man to keep the wedding party small. She worried that he was compromising too much for her, but he assured her it didn't matter to him.

"I guess I'm going to make kind of a grand entrance tomorrow," Samantha told Talia. "Everyone should be here and seated already. Kathy and I won't come into the hall until we're about to begin. Then she'll walk out and we'll play the bridal march before I come out and make my grand entrance, I guess."

She wasn't a huge fan of being the center of attention, but she decided to soak up the moment for her wedding. It would bring memories for her to remember and maybe tell to her daughter one day, if she had one. Absently, she touched her stomach.

"Are you feeling okay?" Talia asked. "Nerves?"

Samantha nodded politely and waved Kathy over.

"Why don't I trade places with her?" Talia suggested and stepped over to help Steven lay out the tablecloths on the remaining tables.

Kathy walked over and flashed a bright smile. "This is exciting! It's actually happening!"

"Yeah," Samantha said without a hint of excitement in her voice. "You said the flowers are coming tomorrow morning?"

As a way to compromise with Mary on the venue, Samantha agreed to an outrageous number of flowers to freshen up the fire hall. Mary and Marty were footing the bill, so Samantha didn't mind. Besides, if she was being honest with herself, she knew the flowers *would* brighten up the drab space.

"Yup," Kathy said with a nod. "The florists are going to

bring them first thing in the morning so they're fresh. I've already explained to Steven, Robert, and Marty where we want everything to go. Cross your fingers that there aren't any hiccups. If worse comes to worst, they can always call us at the house."

"And we'll be at the house with the hairdressers?"

Again, Kathy nodded. "Yes. And the girl who is doing our makeup will be there at ten. By time either me or Mary gets done with our hair, we should be able to start right on makeup and then get into our dresses."

As a show of good faith, Samantha had also invited Mary to participate in a lot of the bridal party events. Not that there was much of a bridal party, but she could tell it made both Steven and Mary happy to see her making an effort.

"Oh no! The dresses! I was supposed to pick them up from the dry cleaners!" Samantha tucked her hair behind her ears.

"I already took care of it," Kathy said. "I took the bus to Steven's office downtown today and borrowed his car to pick up the dresses—and the tuxes. Everything is where it should be and it's all ready for tomorrow."

Samantha let out another deep breath. "Thanks, Kathy. I really appreciate it."

"Hey, being between semesters has given me time to get all of this running around done," Kathy said. She had just finished her first semester at Porreco College and was about to start her second in another week. "Good job picking a wedding date."

Samantha smirked. "Okay, here's another curveball: what about catering?"

"They're getting here around one. They're going to enter through the kitchen door so we shouldn't hear them at all." She turned and pointed to the counter with a window looking into the kitchen. "They're going to lay all the food out there, so when we're ready to eat, they should just lift the doors and we'll be on our way. It'll make clean-up for them easier too."

"Okay," Samantha said with a nod.

"Anything else you want to double check?"

Samantha's stomach rumbled. "Yeah, what about dinner tonight? I'm hungry."

"I ordered subs from a deli not too far from here," Kathy said. "I got you a turkey club, with light mayo, no pickles. Chip, from the fire department, offered to go get them for us about twenty minutes ago. He should be back anytime now."

Samantha smiled. "When did you get so responsible?"

"I'm just taking my maid of honor duties very seriously."

"Sam, do we have anymore of these candles?" Steven called from across the room. "I think we're one or two short."

"There should be another package of them in the bag I brought," she called back.

"Your purse?"

"No! Hold on." She walked across the room and pulled out a shopping bag from beneath her coat, which was laying on the stack of tables they hadn't used. "Here, I picked some up on my way over." She pointed to the carts that held the tables. "We're going to do something with these, right?"

"Chip said there's room to stash them in the storage closet," Marty told her. "We'll make this place look as best as it can be, don't you worry."

Mary scoffed as she laid out the last of the solomon's seal flowers, but Samantha ignored her.

The front door opened and sent a brisk chill through the room. Chip closed the door behind him and held up a plastic bag.

"Food's here!" he declared.

"Thanks for running out to get those." Samantha stepped toward him with her wallet in hand. "What do I owe you?"

"Don't worry about—"

Behind her, Mary let out a scream and Kathy called out, "Talia!"

Samantha spun around and saw the officiant writhing on the floor. Only the whites of her eyes showed and spittle foamed from her mouth. Robert sunk down beside her immediately and cradled her head.

"Call 9-1-1!" Samantha told Chip. He ran into the office.

Samantha stepped forward and watched as the woman she'd been talking to not ten minutes earlier was now having a full-on seizure on the floor. Selfishly, she hoped this wasn't a bad omen for what was to come.

CHAPTER 3

Casandra bagged up an ounce of jasmine into a bag for Brittany, one of her regular customers. She didn't seem like someone who would come to an occult shop—from her bright blonde hair that smelled of hairspray to her limp wrist extended above where her purse sat at the crook of her elbow—but she was in once or twice a month getting an assortment of herbs. And she knew more than she let on about all the things in the shop. Cassandra had heard her help another customer when it was busy in the shop last October.

Meanwhile, another customer—someone completely new—perused the bookshelves at the back of the shop. He was a quiet-looking man with short-cropped hair and thick glasses. He kept his hands deep in the pockets of his thick winter coat as he read through the titles.

"Are you having trouble sleeping?" Cassandra asked Brittany as she tied a ribbon around the bag of herbs—silver ribbon, to bring peace and divinity.

"Yeah, I've been having nightmares," she said. "I'm hoping this will help me better than the drugs my doctor keeps trying to prescribe me. I just don't like taking a lot of pills, you know?"

Cassandra nodded and passed the bag to her. "Trust me, I know. Next time you make tea, add these leaves to the bottom of the strainer and run your hot water through for your tea. I promise you, it'll help you sleep."

Brittany smiled. "That was my plan. I've already tried some incense, but I don't want to do too much. I'm hoping this insomnia is temporary."

"Good luck and sleep well." Cassandra waved as Brittany exited the shop into the cold evening.

Turning, Cassandra sealed up the container where they kept the herbs and set it back under the register. As she pulled away, something appeared in a flash of light in the shelf beside the container.

It was a book—an old one. Leather-bound and scratched. The pages had yellowed with age and were all unevenly trimmed.

She stared at it a moment. Where had it come from? And why was it here?

The man by the bookshelves coughed and her eyes flickered

up to the last customer in the shop.

Crossing to the back of the store, Cassandra approached him. "Is there something I can help you with?"

He snapped around nervously, his face immediately going red. "Well, um…I don't know—I guess I'm just looking."

"Is there something in particular you're looking for?"

"It's stupid. My girlfriend is into astrology and I thought you might have something about it."

Her face lit up. "Oh, sure! We have a bunch of books about that. All down here on the bottom shelf." She stepped over to the second bookshelf and crouched down to pull out some options. "Is there something in particular she likes? Phases of the moon? Alignment of the planets? Constellations?

"Um…constellations, I think?" He sounded unsure. "She's really into signs and all that. She thinks her whole life was predetermined by the fact that she's a sagittarius."

Cassandra smiled and grabbed the book about constellations. "Ah, I see. This book explains the backgrounds behind those meanings and how the constellations were discovered and given meaning to. It's actually quite interesting and perhaps it's something you might want to take a look at for yourself."

He took the book from her but shook his head. "Nah, this isn't really my thing."

"But if it's something she enjoys, perhaps you owe it to her to see into her world a bit?"

He rocked his head back and forth. "I guess that's true. How much is this?"

She told him the price and he said he'd take it. She led him back to the register, where she immediately felt growing unease. The sudden appearance of that mysterious book didn't feel right, but she wanted the shop to be empty before she explored it.

The man paid for the book and Cassandra bagged it up for him and followed him to the door. Once he was back on the sidewalk, she flipped the "OPEN" sign over and locked the door.

Slowly, Cassandra retreated behind the counter again to inspect the book. It seemed to be radiating a dark presence and she was afraid to touch it, to even bump into it.

Grabbing a ceremonial cloth from the counter, she grabbed ahold of the thick tome and wrapped it tightly in the cloth, careful not to lay a finger on it. Carrying it to a back table where it was less likely to be touched, Cassandra took several careful steps away from it.

She let out a deep breath and gave a quick glance to the door before returning her attention to the book.

"Hurry home, Talia," she muttered to herself. "I have no idea what we've gotten ourselves into."

TO READ THE REST OF **SORCERER**,
ORDER YOUR COPY AT
DAVIDNETHBOOKS.COM/COVEN

More by the Author

To find more books by the author, visit
DavidNethBooks.com/Books

* * *

Subscribe to his newsletter to be the first to know of new
releases and special deals!
DavidNethBooks.com/Newsletter

* * *

If you enjoyed the book, please consider leaving a review
on Goodreads or the retailer you bought it from. Reviews
help potential readers determine whether they'll enjoy a
book, so any comments on what you thought of the story
would be very helpful!

About the Author

David Neth is the author of the Coven series, the Under the Moon series, Heat series, the Fuse series, and other stories. He lives in Batavia, NY, where he dreams of a successful publishing career and opening his own bookstore.

Also writes small town romance as D. Allen.

www.DavidNethBooks.com

www.facebook.com/DavidNethBooks